THE ASSASSIN'S PRAYER

THE ASSASSINS
BOOK 1

MARK ALLEN

ROUGH
EDGES
PRESS

ALSO BY MARK ALLEN

Lucas Stone/Primal Justice Series

Fury Divine

Bad Samaritan

Killing Creed

Unchained Vengeance

Reaper Series

Kane: Tooth & Nail (Fear the Reaper Book 1)

Kill Count

This one's for Gerry. Thanks for being my sidekick.

THE ASSASSIN'S PRAYER

AS HE ENTERED Ardee's Diner & Truck Stop, Gabriel Asher spotted Silas Kurto seated in a booth in the back, as far away as possible from the truckers sitting at the counter munching their way through plates of bacon, eggs, and home fries. It probably annoyed the waitress that she would have to walk all the way to the back of the diner to wait on them, but judging from the way the wrinkled uniform stretched across her ample paunch and thighs, she could use the extra exercise. Didn't much matter to him whether she liked it or not and he was pretty sure Silas didn't care either.

He fought back the conflicting emotions he always felt when he was in Silas' presence, the wrenching sensation of hate and friendship, at war with each other like a couple of mangy mutts trying to decide who's going to get the bone. He clamped down on the feelings, pushed them back into the shadows where they belonged. Right now was all about business. The sins of the past would have to wait.

The door closed behind him, hinges creaking in metallic protest. The waitress approached, grease staining her uniform, time staining her rather plain face. "Take a seat wherever you like," she said, her voice dripping with that *I-don't-give-a-crap* drawl used by cynics the world over.

"Thanks." Asher made his way through the tables scattered across the floor in no discernible pattern. He felt the furtive stares of the truckers watching him, the natives checking out the stranger in their midst, and a hard knot of tension prickled between his shoulder blades.

Relax. Even if someone here tries to go all ape-shit on your ass, you're ready for it. He'd left a sawed-off shotgun under the seat in his Jeep, but beneath his long black duster, a .45-caliber Heckler & Koch HK45 Tactical semi-automatic pistol rode in shoulder leather. He also had a Gerber Guardian Back Up dagger tucked into his right boot. Not quite enough hardware to jump-start World War III, but more than enough to turn the diner into a kill-zone if need be.

He slid into the booth across from Silas. He didn't say hello or nod or offer any kind of greeting whatsoever.

Silas leaned forward, the overhead lights gleaming on his shaved skull. He plucked an electronic cigarette from between his lips and exhaled a cloud of water vapor. "You made me wait," he said. "You know I hate waiting."

"If you're looking for someone that cares, you came to the wrong place." Asher pointed at the cigarette. "Got another one of those?"

"It's an electronic cigarette. Why would I have more than one? Besides, I thought you quit."

"I did, but being around you leaves a bad taste in my mouth. Kind of like someone rubbed dog shit all over my tongue. Thought a cigarette might get rid of it."

Silas ignored the jab and took another drag as he glanced around the diner. Just your typical grease-pit with wallpaper that had been outdated when Elvis was jailhouse rocking, a souvenir counter crammed full of cheap gadgets and worthless trinkets, and a floor that, while not exactly filthy, you wouldn't want to eat off.

Silas shook his head. "I don't get it, Gabriel. Why do you insist on living up here in cow country? You're over four hours from the city. Can't be too many job opportunities around here for people in your profession." He exhaled a plume of fake smoke. "And why are we meeting in this shithole?"

"I'd rather gouge my eyes out with a rusty fork than live in the city," Asher replied. "And we're meeting here because it's quiet, anonymous, and supposedly makes a killer western omelet."

"How can you hate the Big Apple? People come from all over the world to visit New York City. But you, just a few hours away, avoid it like leprosy." Silas shook his head. "I don't get it."

"I just prefer the country, that's all."

A waitress approached. Not the large-hipped cynic; this one was younger, prettier, her face unmarked by time's passage or cynicism's bite. Asher tried to remember back to a time when he had been that fresh-faced and innocent. It was damn hard. Felt like he had been on the killing fields forever.

"Sorry, sir," she said to Silas, "but there's no smoking in here."

"It's not real."

"Then what's the point?"

Silas grunted. "I hear that."

"Coffee?" The waitress hefted the carafe in her hand. She had a warm smile and a cheery voice.

Asher slid his cup over to her. "Sure."

"How 'bout some breakfast, boys?"

"Just the coffee for me, thanks," Silas replied.

"Heard you're famous for your westerns," Asher said.

"Famous might be stretching things a bit," the waitress said with a grin, "but it's better than a kick in the nuts."

"With that kind of glowing recommendation, how can I say no?"

She jotted down the order and whisked away.

When she was gone, Asher looked at Silas. "Let's get down to business. I don't want to be around you any longer than I have to."

Silas sighed. "What happened to us, Gabe?" Regret filled his voice.

"You know damn well what happened."

"So I guess forgiveness isn't on today's agenda, huh?"

"Not today. Not ever. Now let's finish our business so you can go back to leaving me the fuck alone."

Silas clearly wanted to push the issue, but Asher's cold stare made him reconsider. He shrugged and said, "Fine, suit yourself." He reached into his jacket, took out a plain white envelope, and slid it across the table. "There's the target info, plus ten grand."

"Numbers?"

"Five. Target plus four guards."

"You're forty grand shy."

Silas nodded, sucked on his e-cigarette again, and let the water vapor trickle out to curl around his face like swamp fog. "You know Frank's good for it. Consider this a down payment and you can collect the rest upon completion of the job. That work for you?"

"I'll live with it."

"Good." Silas stood up. "Next time we meet, we do it down in the city, not up here where sodomizing pigs and strumming banjos are popular pastimes. And we do it at a decent hour, not the crack of dawn." He gestured out the window. "It's not even light yet, for God's sake."

"Maybe I like the dark."

"Of course you like the dark. Hides your sins."

"We're all sinners."

Silas rolled his eyes. "I'm outta here. You start talking like a damn priest, you make me nervous."

"What's the matter, Silas? Afraid of salvation?"

There was pain in Silas' eyes and a longing for something lost. "Gabriel," he said, "did you ever stop to consider that maybe *you're* the one who needs salvation, not me?" With that, he turned and walked away.

The waitress brought his western. Turned out she was right—it was better than a kick in the nuts, but not by much. Asher polished it off anyway and then nursed his cup of coffee—which was strong enough to jump-start a dead mule—as he opened the envelope. Inside were several photos of his next target, Peter Perelli, a middle-aged man whose black hair had just started going gray. Perelli was a mid-echelon player in New

York City's organized crime ranks, making a name for himself in drugs and prostitution.

Asher had been expecting this job. Asher's client, Frank Giadello, was an up-and-comer in the shadow world of organized crime and the best way to rise to the top quickly was to eliminate the competition. Having Perelli killed was a power play for Frank.

Of course, this power play came trimmed with some personal overtones. Last week Perelli had hijacked a shipment of coke meant for the Giadello organization. If Frank let such a blatant insult go unchallenged, he was finished. Perelli had flexed his muscles, so Asher had been hired to slap him down and send a message through the criminal ranks that Frank Giadello was not to be crossed.

He would not have to travel far. Perelli owned a country estate in Hartford, a small farming community twenty miles to the east, not far from where Asher had grown up. According to the stats sheet, Perelli was something of a recluse who preferred the smell of dung and silage to that of exhaust fumes and factories, the tranquility of wide open spaces to the hustle and bustle of metropolitan chaos. A man after Asher's own heart.

He drained the last dregs of coffee, put the photo and stats sheet in his pocket, and then pulled the thick bundle of cash out of the envelope. Seemed like a lot of money...until you considered it was the price of a man's life.

I'm not killing innocents. I'm not gunning down babies or popping slugs between little old ladies' eyes. All I'm doing is exterminating scum. Peter Perelli is a piece of trash who deserves to die.

The same excuses he used every time, an internal ritual of self-justification.

They were cold comfort.

————

Moonlight filtered through the clouds and striated the night sky as Asher turned off Route 40 onto County Route 30 at the base of Rowe Hill. Eighteen hours had passed since he had received the target package from Silas. Between preparations for tonight's strike, he had spent more time than he cared to admit thinking about the past, reliving the good times he and Silas had shared growing up. Looking at them now, nobody would ever believe they had once been the best of friends. People rarely understood the fragility of friendship; sometimes all it takes is a single sin to shatter even the strongest of bonds.

He parked his Jeep Wrangler Sahara in a weed-choked lot that had once been a Post Office but was now just a remote rendezvous for local kids looking to get drunk, get high, get laid, or some combination thereof. Evidence of carnality littered the ground; broken beer bottles, condom wrappers, and even syringes crackled under his boots.

The black duffel bag in the back of the Jeep contained the various items required to complete this hit. Perelli's walled estate perched on the crest of Rowe Hill, overlooking the village of Hartford like the fortress of some medieval tyrant. Dressed in black fatigues, Asher slung the bag over his shoulder and ghosted into the woods, flowing like dark water through the underbrush as he made the steep, half-mile trek to the top of the hill. The night air, crisp with the kiss of autumn, cooled the perspiration that dewed his face, which he had painted with black stripes to help him melt into the shadows.

Pine trees rimmed the northern perimeter of Perelli's estate, providing Asher the cover he needed to get close. But not too close; a drive-by reconnaissance earlier this afternoon had revealed surveillance cameras mounted along the wall every fifty yards. Safe to assume that the cameras fed into a monitor room manned by at least one of Perelli's thugs. Which meant one of the cameras needed to be blinded before he made his move.

He crouched in the deep shadows of the pines, opened the duffel bag, and withdrew a CO_2-powered air rifle and a stash of paintball pellets. With an efficiency bred by a lifetime of handling weapons, he loaded the gun and then moved toward the edge of the trees. He positioned himself behind the trunk of a large pine and braced the rifle against his shoulder. Peering through the sights as he waited for the nearest camera to pan back in his direction, Asher took several deep breaths to steady his muscles. It was a relatively close shot but the air rifle was not a precision weapon.

The camera swung his way. Asher fired, the sound of the shot nothing more than a soft pop. The pellet struck the camera lens and splattered it with black paint, blinding the electronic eye. Asher quickly stowed the gun back in the bag. Anyone manning the monitors would soon notice one of the cameras had gone dark. Guards would be dispatched to investigate. No time to waste.

He peeled away from the cover of the pines and

raced to the wall, ten feet of brick capped with six inches of concrete. He executed a flawless parkour move, placing his right foot against the bricks and surging upward in one fluid motion. His hands hooked the top of the wall and pulled, increasing his momentum, carrying him up and over. He landed on the other side, boots sinking into the lush, well-manicured lawn. The automatic sprinklers had showered the grass recently and moonlight danced on the droplets.

Shouts of alarm sounded from the house. He froze for a moment, crouched like a predator in the shadow of the wall. Adrenalin pumped hot and fast through his veins as he realized they had discovered the crippled camera sooner than anticipated. Time to throw stealth out the window and get ready to play rough, because this strike was about to go hard.

He drew his sound-suppressed HK45 from its shoulder holster. The stats sheet had warned that a pair of attack-trained Dobermans guarded Perelli's grounds. They would be the first to arrive and Asher would have no choice but to put them down.

They barreled out of the shadows moments later, fangs bared, ears pasted flat to their skulls, throats brimming with angry snarls. They began to bark furiously, letting their handlers know they had cornered the intruder.

Asher leveled the HK and pulled the trigger. The .45 slug hammered the first dog dead into the ground.

He swung his pistol toward the second Doberman. But before he could fire, a spotlight blazed to life, pinning him in its harsh white glare. He heard someone shout, "Over there! By the wall!"

He dove to the left as gunfire rocked the night.

Bullets blistered the space he had occupied a heartbeat before. He heard the sizzling smack of ricochets pocking the wall.

"Get the light on him!"

The second Doberman slammed into Asher's chest. They went down in a tangled heap. The dog snapped at his face like it was a tasty delicacy he wanted to tear off and gobble down, splattering him with hot drool. Asher grabbed the animal's throat with his left hand, keeping the sharp teeth momentarily at bay.

"Over there! I think the dogs got him!"

The circle of light from the spot-lamp swept across the grass, searching, probing, seeking. Asher knew he only had a few seconds to get clear of the Doberman. If the light pinned him while he was still wrestling with the dog, it was game over.

His left hand still locked like a vise on the animal's throat, Asher used his right to jam the muzzle of the .45 under the dog's front leg. The Doberman shuddered as the bullet blew through its heart.

Asher shoved the canine corpse aside and regained his feet as the spotlight swept inexorably toward him. He slid the HK back into shoulder leather and drew a short-barreled Franchi SPAS-12 semi-auto combat shotgun from his duffel bag.

A microsecond before the spotlight nailed him, Asher fired a blast of buckshot that blew out the light in a spray of sparks and glass. Darkness returned and Asher welcomed it. In this deadly game of hunter and prey, light was the enemy, darkness an ally. His years of training had conditioned Asher to maneuver better at night than most men did at high noon.

As the shattered spot-lamp winked out, Asher saw

three shadows crouched beside the wrecked machine. Two of the figures detached themselves from the other and circled around back of the house.

Asher ghosted in a wide arc around the remaining guard, wanting to take him from behind. The thick grass hushed his footsteps as he edged toward the man like a shark on a blood scent. He stalked close enough to smell the guard's cheap cologne and hear his raspy breathing when the radio on the man's belt crackled to life.

"Patrol One, this is Johnson. Come in. Over."

As the guard reached for the radio, Asher mentally pulled up the information on Johnson, Perelli's chief of security. Johnson was a black man who tipped the scales at about two-sixty and judging from the photos Asher had viewed, all of it was solid muscle. He bragged twenty years' experience in executive body guarding and had spent the last five employed by Peter Perelli, acquiring substantial wealth in the process.

Asher hoped the money spent in hell, because with this strike royally pooch-screwed, there was no doubt that he would have to go through Johnson to get to Perelli.

The guard thumbed his radio, oblivious to Asher's lethal presence right behind him. "This is Patrol One. Go ahead, boss."

"Give me a sit-rep." Johnson's voice crackled with radio static.

"We lost the target when he took out the light. Guy's packing some serious heat."

"Where are Patrols Two and Three?"

"Out back looking for this asshole."

"I don't want to hear *looking*, I want to hear *found*. Got it?"

"Ten-four, boss. We'll keep looking."

Asher nudged the nape of the guard's neck with the shotgun. "You can stop looking. You found me."

The man stiffened, but made no attempt to turn around, smart enough to know he had just been checkmated.

"Toss your weapon," Asher commanded.

The guard complied.

"Now call the others back here."

The guard asked, "Who are you?"

Asher caught the quiver in the man's voice. Hard to be a tough guy when you're riding the wrong end of a twelve-gauge. "Just do what you're told."

The guard raised the radio to his lips. "Patrols Two and Three, this is One. Come in. Over."

A burst of static, then: "This is Two. Three's standing by."

"Return to my position ASAP."

"Ten-four, on our way."

The guard lowered the radio. "I just helped you kill two of my friends."

"Friends are overrated," Asher said.

"Sounds like you need a therapist."

"And you need a coroner." Asher triggered the shotgun. The guard's skull exploded. The headless corpse flopped face down on the grass in a twitching heap. Working fast, Asher plucked a fragmentation grenade from his bag of tricks and pulled the pin. He carefully lodged the fragger underneath the body so the dead weight kept the arming spoon from popping up. He then snatched up the dead guard's radio and ducked around the corner of the house just as the two other gunmen rounded the opposite corner. He watched and listened from the shadows as they crouched down beside their deceased comrade.

"Shit, man, he's dead!" one of them said. "The bastard killed him!"

"That's an understatement," the other replied. "His whole damn head's gone!" He grabbed one of the corpse's arms. "Help me roll him over."

Neither of them saw the grenade in time. They both vanished in a volcano of smoke and fire, shredded by shrapnel from soles to scalps. The concussive blast imploded the large bay window nearby, spraying glass into Perelli's living room.

The radio Asher had hijacked squawked to life. "Patrol One, this is Johnson. Someone want to tell me what the hell is going on out there?"

Asher pressed the radio to his lips and keyed the mic. "Death," he said quietly. Sure, it was overdramatic and cheesy as a Chuck Norris movie, but messing with the enemy's mind never hurt. A little psychological warfare could yield a critical edge when the bullets started bouncing all over the place.

There was only silence from the other end. A full ten seconds ticked by before the radio crackled again. "Who is this?" Johnson demanded. "And what do you want?"

"I've got a white rose to give to your boss." The white rose was Asher's signature, a ritual he started five years ago, following the death of his wife. Anyone involved in the criminal underworld would recognize his calling card.

Apparently Johnson did, for after another long pause he said, "*Asher?*"

"Buckle up, Johnson. This ride is about to get bumpy." Asher dropped the radio to the ground and stomped it to pieces.

The time to talk was over.

Now it was time to kill.

Asher stepped over the three shredded sacks of blood and guts sprawled lifelessly in front of the house and entered through the shattered bay window. He found himself standing in a large family room. Plush wall-to-wall carpet covered the floor beneath the mess of broken glass. A marble coffee table provided the room's centerpiece around which was arranged black leather furniture with chrome trim. To his right, Asher saw a large entertainment center recessed into the oak-paneled wall, complete with a flat-screen TV so massive it could have doubled as the movie screen at a drive-in theater. A large ceiling fan dangled overhead, the bamboo blades hanging motionless.

He tensed as a sudden yowl sounded from somewhere nearby. He heard a young girl cry out, "Purry! No!" followed by the telltale patter of someone running on bare feet. Whoever it was, they were coming his way. Asher dropped to one knee and aimed the SPAS-12 at the living room's only entrance.

A woman, voice raw with terror, screamed someone's name. "*AMYYYYYY!*"

Asher's combat senses redlined as the footsteps came closer.

His finger curled around the trigger, taking up the slack.

A black and white streak rocketed through the doorway. Amped up on adrenalin, Asher almost blew the cat into a red smudge but caught himself at the last moment. The feline skittered along the back of the leather sofa and vanished beneath the antique piano in the far corner of the room.

A second later, a little girl ran into the room, crying, *"Purry!"* She jumped onto the couch and scrambled toward the other end, calling for her pet. Right behind came a woman wearing only a short, filmy nightgown that did little to hide her curvaceous body. She didn't even look at Asher; just lunged across the sofa after the little girl. The short gown slid up over her waist, exposing the kind of perfectly heart-shaped ass that makes men salivate.

It was almost Asher's last sight on earth. With images of satin buttocks dancing on his retinas, he nearly missed movement on his peripheral. He threw himself sideways as Johnson spun into the entrance and fired his Glock-19 in one smooth, well-practiced motion. Asher felt the slug sizzle past his ear. He hit the floor, landing hard on his shoulder. Broken glass dug at him but the pain barely registered. He had more pressing needs. Like not having his internal organs scrambled by a bullet.

Still skidding along the carpet, he triggered the shotgun and took out Johnson's legs, churning everything below the knees into splintered pulp. Johnson went down like a cut-string marionette, screaming in pain. Huddled on the couch, the woman pressed the little girl's face to her chest.

As he climbed to his feet and stalked toward Johnson, Asher felt the familiar iciness seep through him, leaching away concepts like compassion, sympathy, and mercy. Right now, with the pungency of blood and gunpowder polluting the air, there was no room for such emotions.

The crackle and crunch of glass under his boots sounded ominous in the unnatural quiet that had settled over the house in the wake of all this violence. The woman softly whimpered but she was nothing more than background noise and he ignored her. Scared out of her mind, she was way too frightened to try anything, especially with the kid clutched in her arms.

Despite the agony of his buckshot amputation, Johnson still made a game attempt to raise his Glock as the assassin approached. Asher kicked it out of his hand. He could smell Johnson's fear, a sour rankness seeping from his pores. Few men could stare into the Reaper's eyes without flinching, and as it turned out, Johnson was not one of those few. "Please," he blubbered, "don't kill me, man. I'm begging you."

Asher had expected better from Johnson. The man had spent the last twenty years living by the gun and should have known that when you play with guns, you're bound to eventually eat a bullet. Asher himself suffered no delusion that he would die peacefully in his bed of old age; when his time came, he would go down hard and bloody on the killing field. That's just the way it was.

Asher's cold gaze raked Johnson's face as if scouring skin from skull. "Suck it up, fella. It's your turn to dance with the devil." He pressed the muzzle of the SPAS-12 right over Johnson's frantically-beating heart.

Johnson closed his eyes. "Oh, God, I don't wanna die."

"Who does?" Asher said as he pulled the trigger.

Johnson's chest came apart like a blood-stuffed piñata whacked by a wrecking ball. The point blank impact smashed him flat on his back so that his dead eyes stared up at the ceiling.

With that particular threat neutralized, Asher turned toward the woman and child huddled on the sofa. Who were they? They had not been listed on the stats sheet. The young girl appeared to be five or six, her rumpled My Little Pony pajamas indicating she had been sleeping. The woman looked to be in her late thirties. Her large, doe-like eyes gazed at him in shock and fear. By any man's standards, she was beautiful, her oval face framed by sleep-tousled dark brown hair. Her negligee was so scant and filmy that she might as well have been wearing nothing.

As Asher walked over to them, the woman clutched the little girl even closer and tried to shrink into the sofa as if hoping some magical door would open up and whisk them away from this nightmare. "Please," she said as Asher towered over her, shotgun still in his fist, "don't hurt us."

Asher canted the shotgun over his shoulder, pointed away from the two huddled, miserable, quivering creatures on the couch. "Who are you?" he asked.

"I'm Rene Perelli," the woman said. "This is my daughter Amy."

Peter Perelli's wife and kid. Why hadn't they been listed on the stat sheet?

Amy lifted her cherubic face from her mother's chest and peeked out at Asher with frightened eyes. "Are you gonna hurt us, mister?"

Asher ignored her and looked at Rene. "Where is he?"

"Who?"

"Don't even try to play dumb. You know why I'm here."

Rene stroked her daughter's curls comfortingly. "How much are they paying you? What's the going rate for a man's life these days?"

Asher's voice was hard as bullets as he rasped, "You don't tell me where your husband is, your little girl is going to grow up without a mother." It was a bluff—Asher would slit his own throat before harming a woman or child—but Rene didn't know that. For all she knew, he would drop the hammer on her as easy as flushing a goldfish down the toilet.

Desperate tears dripped down her cheeks. "And if I do tell you, she'll grow up without a father. Please, just walk away. Whatever they're paying you, Peter will double it."

Asher had heard the pitch dozens of times before. He stared at her, stoic, waiting.

"There must be something you want! Something that will make you walk away!" Rene was on the verge of a total breakdown, holding it together through nothing more than sheer willpower and that appeared to be fraying fast.

Time to up the ante on his bluff. Asher whipped the shotgun off his shoulder. Pressed it under her chin, forcing her head up. "The only thing I want," he said, "is your husband." He felt like shit, making this innocent woman squirm on the end of his gun. Her choked sobs ripped at his conscience. "Where is he?"

"Right here, you son of a bitch," someone said and gunfire filled the room.

Asher hurled himself backward the instant the first

syllable left Peter Perelli's lips. The bullet sailed by Asher's face, close enough for him to feel the disruption of air as it passed. He landed on his back and swung the SPAS-12 toward Perelli as the mobster frantically tried to reacquire him in the sights of his pearl-handled .38 revolver.

Asher triggered the shotgun. Buckshot slammed into the wood molding framing the doorway in which Perelli stood. Slivers exploded everywhere. Several of them found Perelli's flesh, slashing open a dozen small cuts on his face and neck.

Perelli snarled in pain and fired a wild shot. The bullet clipped the corner of the coffee table and ricocheted into the arm of the sofa, mere inches from where his wife and daughter cowered. Perelli fired again and again, wild and reckless, flinging lead with no regard for the innocents in the room, endangering his own family.

Asher ended the mobster's panicked spray-and-pray antics with another shotgun blast, blowing the revolver into scrap metal and tearing his hand to dripping red tatters.

"*DAAADDDYYYY!*" Amy pulled away from her mother and ran to her father. She wrapped her tiny arms around his waist and as Asher climbed to his feet, he saw blood on her pajamas. This kid was going to need some serious therapy after tonight. She looked at Asher with tearfully bewildered eyes. "Don't hurt my daddy anymore."

Asher slung the shotgun over his shoulder, drew his HK45, and locked eyes with Perelli. "Get her out of the way."

"Please." Blood streamed from Perelli's mangled hand. "I have a family."

"I saw how much you care about your family when you were chucking bullets all over the place a minute ago. Won't tell you again, Perelli—get your kid out of the way."

Perelli searched Asher's eyes, but whatever he sought—mercy, hope, salvation—he apparently didn't find. He looked down at his daughter. "Go to Mommy, honey." He sounded resigned, broken.

Amy balked, hugging him tighter. "No! I don't want to! I want to stay with you!"

"You can't, honey. Go to Mommy."

Asher glanced at Rene. She hadn't moved from her position on the couch. Tears spilled down her face as she looked at her husband with anguished eyes.

Amy reluctantly peeled herself away from her father and returned to her mother. The look she gave Asher was that of a little kid who has not gotten her way. Were the tears dappling her dimpled cheeks tantrum-tears or grief-tears? Did she grasp the severity of the situation? Did she understand she was about to lose her father forever?

Asher wanted out of here. He kept his gaze fixed on Perelli but he could feel Rene and Amy's accusing eyes on him. The sensation made his flesh crawl. He felt like they could somehow stare through his flesh and bones and see the aching, blood-drenched hollow that was his soul. Time to finish the game.

He pressed the end of the pistol's suppressor against Perelli's forehead. It would be quick and clean. Well, maybe not clean. Little hard to be clean with a .45 at point blank range.

"Please," Perelli's voice trembled. "You don't have

to do this. Let me set things right. Tell Giadello I'll make it up to him."

"Little late for that."

"What about my little girl? She'll grow up without a father."

"Guess you should have made smarter life choices."

"You're one cold-hearted son of a bitch."

"Yeah," Asher said, and pulled the trigger.

The suppressor reduced the shot to a muffled cough, but Amy and Rene jumped as if the gun had fired at full roar. Rene let out a horrible cry and hid Amy's face against her breast.

The bullet blew through Perelli's skull and slammed his body backward. He hung there for a moment, crucified to the wall, then slumped to the floor in a sitting position at Asher's feet, head hanging with chin on chest. Blood dribbled into his lap.

"You heartless bastard!" Rene sobbed. She looked as if she had aged twenty years in the last five minutes. "How could you?"

Good question. Asher didn't know how he did what he did. He just did it and then tried his best to ignore the demons that forever howled inside him. And when those questions got too loud to ignore, a bottle of Jack Daniels usually did a fine job of shutting them up.

He reached into his pocket, took out a white rose with crumpled petals, and dropped it onto Perelli's body. It floated through the air like a feather from an angel's wing. When it landed, the white petals turned red as Perelli's blood seeped into them.

Asher walked away without a backward glance. He didn't want to see the grieving face of the woman he had just widowed. He did not want to look into the helpless eyes of the little girl he had just left fatherless. All he wanted to do was get away from here, away from the lives that were now broken and mangled because of what he had done.

Outside, the night enveloped him in a cool, velvet embrace that offered no comfort. He walked through the darkness that was silent save for the soft sobbing of a heartbroken child. As he hiked back down the hill to his Jeep, he told himself that the tears in his eyes were from the wind, nothing more.

He had never been able to lie to himself worth a damn.

CHAPTER 2

ASHER RENDEZVOUSED with Silas at the same diner two days later. He did not order the same omelet. As before, he set the meet for pre-dawn.

They had the place to themselves this time, but they still sat in the same rear booth. Steam drifted up from a cup of coffee in front of Silas who busily worked his way through a greasy pile of fried eggs and sausage with a ferocity akin to Godzilla tearing through downtown Tokyo.

When he was finished, Silas pushed away his plate. "Well, that hit the spot." He wiped his mouth with a napkin and then asked, "The job done?"

"Wouldn't be here if it wasn't."

"We shouldn't be here anyway. Told you I wanted to meet down in the city this time."

"What you want doesn't mean shit to me."

Silas' eyes narrowed. "Watch your tone, Gabriel. I know you hate my guts, and you have that right, but I don't have to put up with your crap."

Asher noticed the cynical, overweight waitress and

the young, attractive one huddled together by the milk-shake machine. Judging by the way they nervously eyed him and Silas, they weren't discussing the best way to mix malt. The hostility between him and Silas crackled through the diner like hot sparks.

Asher felt his anger rising. "Tell you what, Silas, if you don't want to put up with my crap, I can just put a bullet between your eyes like I should have done a long time ago."

Silas leaned back in his seat. "Gabe, it's been five years. How many times do I have to say I'm sorry?"

"You can say you're sorry until you're six feet under," Asher rasped. "You fucked my wife, you son of a bitch. You were my best friend and you *fucked my wife*. So don't sit there and act like you deserve to be forgiven."

Silas looked pained, as if Asher's harsh words had struck home and struck hard.

"I can't take it back," he said quietly. "If I could, I would, but I can't. But remember, Gabe, it takes two. You forgave Karen, right?"

Horrible memories gnawed at Asher's brain. "Yeah, I forgave her."

"So why her and not me?"

"I loved her."

"And I was your best friend."

"Not the same." Asher clenched his fists as the resurrected memories tore at him like rabid rats. He relived that day, walking into his own bedroom and seeing his wife's legs wrapped around his best friend's waist.

Before that moment, Asher would have thought it impossible to survive the kind of pain that ripped at his heart. He had stood there, paralyzed, shock and horror nailing his feet to the floor as Silas thrust between her splayed thighs again and again, his grunts echoing off the walls.

Asher's eyes had sought Karen's face, wanting—no, *needing*—some kind of connection. Her eyes had been closed, lips parted in a soft moan as her fingers clutched at Silas' sweat-slick body. Then, perhaps alerted by some sixth sense, she opened them and saw Asher standing there. He had watched a rapid-fire series of emotions—shock, horror, grief, sorrow, and yes, love—sweep through her eyes. And then, finally, tears. That was when Asher had turned and walked away, the sound of her sobs chasing him as he fled the scene where love had been betrayed.

He never fully recovered from that day. He tried, but if there had been an insurance company for relationships, the claims adjuster would have written this one off as totaled beyond repair. He and Karen stayed together and made several stumbling attempts to put things back the way they had been, but their home had become a corrupted place stained by sin. Asher had been able to forgive her, but he had never been able to forget. He would have murdered a thousand angels to have that memory erased.

"You want to know something, Silas?" Asher said. "I never made love to Karen again. She wanted to, because in spite of it all we still loved each other, right up until the very end. But every time I tried, all I could see was your face. Bet you didn't know that, did you? You were the last person to ever fuck my wife. Now do you really have the balls to sit there and think you have any right to ask for my forgiveness?"

Silas looked miserable. "No, I don't think I have the right. I just don't understand why you can forgive her but not me."

"Maybe it's just easier to forgive the dead."

"You can't put that on me," Silas said. "I didn't kill her. She took her own life."

"So go slit your wrists like she did," Asher rasped. "Won't make us even, but it's a start."

"That really what you want me to do?"

Asher stared at him, remembering Karen's sliced open veins, wondering if he would feel better if Silas did the same. He shook his head. "No," he growled. "No, you live with it, you son of a bitch." He felt tears stinging his eyes. "We're done talking about this."

"Asher, I really think we should—"

Asher cut him off. "I don't care what you think. This subject is closed. Got it?"

"Yeah, I got it."

"Good. Now where's my money?"

"I don't have it."

"Then who does?"

"Frank. He wants me to bring you back to the city to discuss another job."

"No more jobs until I'm paid for the last one."

"Frank is going to pay you," Silas said, "so chill out. He just wants to discuss this new job with you personally, face to face. Since you would rather stick your dick in a meat grinder than go near the city, he figured the best way to get you down there was to hold your money until you came for it."

Asher wanted to tell Silas to pound salt, that he was not a puppet who would dance to someone else's tune. But nearly all his contracts came from Frank Giadello these days, so telling him to kick rocks would just lead to a significant cash flow reduction. Money might not buy happiness but it made misery more comfortable. "Fine," he said. "Tomorrow. Tell Frank to have my money ready."

"Why not today? It's not even dawn yet. If we left now we could be..." Silas' voice trailed off as he looked at Asher and realized he was wasting his breath. He might as well have been begging a sphinx to crack a smile. "All right," he said. "I'll find a motel and we can leave tomorrow morning."

Asher stood up. "By the way, breakfast is on you."

"Yeah, yeah." Silas reached for his wallet.

As Asher drove home, he thought about the bottle of Jack Daniels in the cupboard. Hopefully there was enough left to silence the ghosts Silas had resurrected.

CHAPTER 3

IT WAS a four-mile drive from the diner to Asher's place on West River Road, a rural route that wound along the Hudson River for ten miles before breaking west toward the town of Gansevoort. As his house—a simple two-story box-style with a garage attached to the northwest side—came into view, the sun peeked over the slate-colored mountains in the distance.

Asher steered the Jeep Wrangler Sahara into the blacktopped driveway and past the two L-shaped flower beds bracing both sides of the entrance. He could remember when Karen's green thumb had made the beds bloom with brilliant bursts of color. Now the flower beds were dead. Just like her.

He parked in the garage and hit the remote to close the door behind him. The garage windows, three small squares of glass, were blacked out. Asher valued his privacy, having about as much use for social interaction as a eunuch has for Viagra. His nearest neighbor lived over a mile down the road. There was a thoroughbred farm nestled a half-mile behind him, but a row of locust trees and a large gulch separated his land from theirs. He would have preferred even more isolation—an island in the middle of a lake, for example—but when they were shopping for a house, Karen had refused to go whole hermit. This place had been their compromise and now that she was gone, he couldn't bring himself to let it go. She still lived here through his memories and if he were to move someplace else, Asher knew he would feel like he had abandoned her. Irrational, sure, but nobody ever said grief was a logical beast.

Inside, the house was clean but Spartan. No point in being a slob, but Asher saw no reason to spruce the place up either. Wasn't like he was going to be entertaining friends in the near future and after Karen's death he no longer bothered with women.

He tossed his keys on the kitchen table that squatted under a single bare bulb like an interrogation table in some old hardboiled detective story and retrieved the Jack Daniels from the cabinet. He didn't bother with the niceties of glass and ice; just slugged it straight from the bottle. Seeing Silas again, reliving the betrayal and Karen's suicide, killing a man in front of his wife and kid...it was all too much to take at once. He took another hit and felt the whiskey sear its way down his throat.

He brought the bottle over to the table, got out his gun-cleaning kit, and began to clean the HK45. He struggled to remember how many men he had killed with this pistol. Thirty? Forty? Fifty? He remembered his first kill as if he had pulled the trigger only yesterday. He had drilled a .45 round right through the bridge of the target's nose, and the internal pressure of the bullet burrowing through his brain had caused the sex trafficker's eyeballs to pop out of their sockets. But for the most part the faces all ran together in meaningless, featureless blobs. Maybe that was a good thing.

He reassembled the Heckler & Koch and turned his attention to the SPAS-12. Manufactured by Franchi, the Special Purpose Assault Shotgun was one of his favorite weapons, capable of semi-auto as well as pump-action. When loaded with nine rounds of double-aught buckshot, it was a formidable close-quarters weapon, more than capable of blowing a man in half. Asher had removed the folding stock, preferring to use just the pistol grip. Easier to conceal when necessary.

Few assassins opted for such heavy firepower. Most hitters preferred .22s, preferably to the back of the head. The diminutive round made a small entry hole and lacked the power to exit the opposite side. Neat, tidy, unspectacular. But that wasn't Asher's way.

Every time he went on a strike, his life was on the line. One mistake, one little lapse in concentration, and the target would put one in Asher's heart instead of vice versa. He used this acute awareness of his own mortality to hone his combat instincts, to keep himself sharp, focused, and alive. Sure, his life was a big pile of shit and skeletons, but what waited on the other side was probably worse. He had spent his life violating the Sixth Commandment and he seriously doubted the angels enjoyed getting chummy with trigger pullers. So, with his ass on the line every time he went out on a hit, Asher wanted all the firepower he could muster.

He took another drink from the bottle, loaded the SPAS-12, and racked a shell into the chamber. He kept every gun in the house topped off. Never knew when enemies might come calling. Better to have a loaded gun and never need it than to need a loaded gun and not have one.

He set the shotgun down on the table and headed for the bathroom. The diner coffee was knocking on his bladder.

Standing in front of the toilet, Asher felt a chill slither down his spine like an ice-cold maggot. No surprise there—a ghost haunted the bathroom. This was where Karen died.

Asher still remembered everything as if it had happened five minutes ago instead of five years. Coming home and seeing the water seeping out from underneath the bathroom door. Kicking the door open and seeing Karen in the overflowing tub, her long hair billowing in the water, red on red, her arms floating limply, bone-deep gashes carved in her wrists, the straight razor lying beside the tub. She had been staring straight ahead and Asher remembered thinking there was something horrible about the way she didn't blink when the bloody water lapped across her wide-open eyes.

Asher finished up and hurried out of the bathroom. He returned to the kitchen table, raised the whiskey bottle to his lips, and sucked it down. Not much left, but hopefully enough to knock him out. Because the last thing he wanted to do was stay awake all day reliving his wife's suicide.

He picked up his Gerber dagger and began working it with a whetstone. As the harsh rasp of steel on stone filled the kitchen, he wondered if it would have been easier to accept Karen's death if she had left a note explaining why she had chosen to take her life. But absent an explanation, he blamed Silas, believing that guilt over their affair had driven her to put a blade to her veins.

Asher's hands began to shake, the knife clinking against the whetstone. Time for another shot. He reached for the Jack Daniels and raised it to his lips.

The bullet came out of nowhere. It punched through the glass patio doors and shattered the bottle in Asher's hand. He threw himself sideways out of the chair as a hail of bullets followed the first. He hit the floor hard on his shoulder, feeling the impact ripple through his muscles as the effects of the whiskey evaporated. Nothing like almost catching a bullet in the teeth to sober you up right quick. His face was drenched with Jack Daniels and his eyes burned from the booze.

Asher couldn't hear the shots. Which meant the gunner was using a suppressor. Which meant a pro. Your average garden variety burglar rarely bothered with a silencer...or full auto firepower for that matter.

More slugs slammed into the table. Asher frantically rubbed at his stinging eyes. Through a blur of tears, he saw the auto-fire fusillade hammer the SPAS-12 into a wreckage of mangled metal. The stream of hot lead tracked toward him, digging holes in the linoleum as Asher rolled, seeking cover. Something hot burned across his calf and then he was behind the island in the center of the kitchen.

His heart raced, pumping with adrenalin. His vision had almost returned to normal. Drops of whiskey dripped from his cheeks. There was a fiery pain just below his right eye where a piece of glass had cut him. Not much worse than a shaving nick, but the alcohol made it sting like hell. Somehow through all the diving, rolling, and scurrying to survive, he had managed to hold onto the dagger. Of course, all that meant was that he had brought a knife to a gunfight.

He heard footsteps coming up the basement stairs and cursed. There were *two* hitters, closing in from opposite angles in a classic pincer ploy. If they caught him in a crossfire he would be ventilated with more holes than a colander collection.

The second hitter kicked open the basement door. Screws screeched in protest as one of the hinges tore loose from the frame. The black-garbed gunman burst into the room in a combat crouch, his Colt M4A1 carbine swiveling toward Asher, seeking target acquisition with the Aimpoint reflex optic.

A dagger is not designed to be a throwing knife, but Asher practiced with it frequently, the distance was short, and he had no other options. With a flick of his wrist, he sent the blade zipping across the room and sank the dagger into the gunner's left eye. The man went down instantly, cold steel impaling his brain, the handle jutting from his socket like some obscene growth. The M4 tumbled from his lifeless fingers.

Asher eyed the Colt carbine and the distance that separated him from it. He wanted that gun. He *needed* that gun. There was still another hitter out there, closing in fast, and the M4 might mean the difference between breathing oxygen and sucking dirt. It was only about ten feet to the gun, a relatively short gap. But in order to cross it, Asher would have to briefly expose himself to the second hitter.

No time for hesitation. His survival chances slimmed with each second he wasted.

He gathered his legs under him and lunged into the open, his adrenalized muscles hurling him across the linoleum like a human cannonball. Bullets plucked at his clothes but missed his skin; he was moving too fast to make an easy target. He snatched up the M4 as momentum carried him through a full roll. He came up on his knees, facing the shattered patio doors, just as the second gunner stormed into the room.

Both men fired simultaneously.

The gunner had expected Asher to rise to his feet, not his knees, so he fired too high. Asher heard the hum of bullets zipping over his head followed by the *thwack-thwack-thwack* sound as they buried themselves in the wall behind him.

Asher aimed lower. *Much* lower. The 5.56mm salvo chopped into the target's shins and then tracked upward, blowing apart his thighs. The thick bones ruptured like hammered ice. He toppled onto his back, the air exploding from his lungs in a whoosh as he hit the floor.

Asher scrambled over and kicked the gun out of the hitter's hands. He thought he heard the man's wrist snap in the process but wasn't sure. He didn't care either. This bastard had tried to kill him.

The gunner tried to sit up. Asher pinned the guy's throat beneath his boot with enough force to keep him down but not hard enough to crush his larynx. He didn't want the man dead. Not yet, anyway. Not until they had a little chat.

Asher didn't recognize the man, but that didn't mean anything. He touched the hot barrel of the carbine to the tip of the man's nose.

"Answer my questions," Asher said, "and you'll live. Refuse and you die. Simple as that. You're a professional, so I'm sure you understand that if you make me put you down, I'll put you down hard. So save yourself the pain, do us both a favor, and talk to me."

It was a good speech, but it didn't work. The gunner kept his mouth closed so tight you would have thought his jaw was wired shut. He stared up at Asher with flat, emotionless eyes that revealed nothing. In fact, those eyes were barely even registering *pain*.

Maybe this guy was Black Talon. Asher had heard rumors that Talon underwent extreme pain-tolerance training. But c'mon, the guy's legs were nothing but hamburger. He had to be feeling *something*.

"Are you Company?" Asher asked.

No reply.

Asher lifted the M4's muzzle off the gunman's nose, pressed it against the spot where the man's left arm hinged to his shoulder, and pulled the trigger. Apparently the man's pain-tolerance techniques did not extend to having his arm nearly amputated by a half-dozen bullets after having his legs blown to shreds—he howled in agony.

During his years with the Company, Asher had encountered operatives who cultivated a taste for torture, who got their rocks off by inflicting prolonged pain upon others, but they had been the demented, the deranged, the sadists and psychopaths. For Asher, torture was just one more tool in the toolbox, something that had to be used sometimes to harvest information. Sure, drugs were better, the information they extracted more reliable—a man being tortured will sell his own mother down the river to stop the pain, making the information gleaned suspect—but Asher didn't have any sodium pentothal sitting in his medicine cabinet. So he would just have to keep pumping bullets into various body parts until the gunner broke.

"Let's try that again." Asher moved the M4 to the gunman's other shoulder. "Are you Company?"

Sweat dappled the man's forehead and rolled down his face. Through agony-clenched teeth he hissed, "They'll kill me if I talk."

"I'll kill you if you don't and I'm right here, right now. Worry about me. Now, one last time—you Company?"

"Yes."

"Talon?"

"Trying."

"What's that supposed to mean?"

"I'm in the program," the man replied. "Last phase. You were my final field test. They sent me to take you out and if I succeeded, I would be part of the Black Talon team."

"You're telling me this hit was nothing more than a training exercise?"

"Basically, yeah."

"Who sent you?"

"Macklin."

Of course. Asher had known this day would come. The Company was not in the habit of letting their top-tier assassins just walk away. He was surprised it took them this long to send a team after him. Wasn't like he had been hiding out or on the run—there was no point. He knew better than most that if the Company wanted to find you, then you would be found, whether you were living as a monk in some Mongolian monastery or simply residing at your last known address. He had simply learned to live with the itch between his shoulder blades, knowing the crosshairs would come eventually.

"Macklin is going to kill you," the crippled gunman said. His face was turning an unhealthy shade of white. Blood pumped from his shattered legs in a widening pool, probably from a bullet-pierced femoral. Add to that the severed arm and the man was living on borrowed time.

Asher took his foot off the man's neck. "Maybe," he said. "But you're going first."

The hitter lifted a hand, the only one that still worked, and rubbed his throat where Asher's boot had pressed. He then lowered it back to his side and looked up at the man he had failed to kill. "Make it quick, will you?"

"Sure." Asher put a triple-burst through the hitter's face.

Next, he called Silas' cell. As it rang, he looked at the piles of dead meat polluting his kitchen and knew the gunner had been right—Macklin would come for him. Two Black Talon protégés were dead and Macklin would take that as both an insult and a challenge.

According to the rumors, myths, legends, and graffiti on the bathroom wall, Black Talon was commanded by a man known only as Colonel Macklin. He wore a wicked ear-to-ear scar on his throat, compliments of the Colombian drug cartels. During a strike against one of their cocaine networks in Bogota, Macklin had been captured and brutally tortured. When the Colombians finally accepted the fact that he simply would not break, they had cut his throat and left him for dead.

But somehow—by making a deal with the devil himself, some whispered—Macklin had survived the ghastly wound. But even though the blade did not kill him, it savaged his larynx, cursing Macklin to the life of a mute. According to the stories, Macklin now hunted in silence, backed by his ruthless band of hand-picked Black Talon operatives.

Black Talon was a black-ops program that was darker than the devil's heart and twice as dangerous, as the saying went among the small circle of Company insiders and Washington power players who knew about its existence. Highly-skilled, lethally-efficient hunter-killer teams and solo operators that did all manner of dirty work and wet jobs across the globe.

Macklin's team specialized in seeking out assassins who tried to leave or whom the Company deemed expendable for whatever reasons. Lay down your guns without permission and eventually Macklin came looking for you. Basically, he was the Company's boogeyman.

Silas answered his phone on the fourth ring. "Hello?"

"I need a cleanup."

"Why?"

"I have two bodies leaking all over my linoleum."

"I've seen that linoleum. The blood is probably an improvement."

"Just get a cleaner over here already."

"Our cleaner is down in the city. Be at least four hours before I can get him to your place. Can you contain the situation for that long?"

"It's already contained. I just need the mess cleaned up."

"Four hours then. If you're not there, my man vanishes."

Four hours turned out to be an optimistic estimate, which left Asher with plenty of time to mull over this morning's events. He knew he had not seen the last of Black Talon. Their reputation for ruthlessly achieving results was well-earned. When the brass pointed at a target, Talon went to work, no questions asked, and didn't stop until that target was terminated. Black bag stuff, off the books; Asher doubted even the president knew about the kill-squad. But any assassin who had ever worked for the Company knew that if you tried to walk away, Talon eventually came calling. Damage control, the brass called it. Silence the slayers, kill the killers, murder the murderers...all part of the Company's cover-your-ass syndrome.

The cleaner arrived shortly after noon, accompanied by Silas, who surveyed the damage in the kitchen and whistled. "They really did a number in here."

"Tell me something I don't know," Asher said.

Silas motioned to the cleaner. "I want your best work, Mr. X. Every single trace of what went down here erased. Got it?"

Mr. X, a middle-aged man with a salt-and-pepper crewcut, looked at Silas with weak eyes that watered so much you'd think he was wearing contact lenses soaked in lemon juice. "When I'm done, this place will be as pure as the Pope's prick."

"Yeah, well, I'm relapsed Catholic and I'm not so sure the Pope's prick doesn't smell like little boys."

Mr. X blinked at him and muttered, "Blasphemer." Then he went to work.

Asher watched the cleaner drag the corpse with the knife in its eye toward the bathroom as Silas leaned against the counter. "Don't let his eyes fool you,

Gabriel. He's tough as nails, gets the job done, and keeps his mouth shut. You got a mess you want cleaned right, Mr. X is the best janitor in the business."

Asher leaned down and plucked the dagger from the cadaver as the cleaner, grunting with exertion, hauled it by. He straightened up and gave Silas a droll look. "Mr. X?"

Silas grinned. "What's in a name, right? Can I help it if the guy's read too many comic books?"

Asher went to the sink and washed the knife as Mr. X disappeared into the bathroom with the body. What came next would be gruesome; Mr. X would douse the bodies with a flesh-dissolving acid. Easier to handle dead men when they're nothing but bones.

Mr. X reappeared to drag the second body into the bathroom.

Silas studied the blood smear left by the corpse as it was dragged away. "Any idea who they were?"

Maybe it was his imagination, but Asher thought he heard a wet sizzling noise coming from the direction of his bathroom. "Company," he said, images of flesh sloughing off skeletons dancing in his head.

Silas whistled. "Guess your past finally came back to bite you, hey, friend?"

"I'm not your friend."

"Think twice before you exile me, Gabe. I mean, take a good look around you." Silas gestured around the room, pointing out the bloodstains and bullet holes like a realtor showing off some new macabre interior design trend called warzone chic. "The Company tried to ice you this morning. That's serious business. Frank has a lot of friends. Powerful friends, politicians, allies in some very high places. I say the word, he makes some calls, and maybe we get high enough up the food chain to make all your problems disappear. Face it, man, you need all the help you can get right now."

Asher wanted another drink, but the bullet-blasted bottle of Jack Daniels had been the only booze in the house. "All I want from Frank is the money he owes me," Asher said. "I'll handle my past my way."

"Gabe, listen to—"

"This conversation is over." Asher headed for his bedroom, passing by the bathroom as he did so. He could hear Mr. X working in there and the smell wafting out was about as pleasant as having your nose rubbed in a dead skunk's rectal cavity. Time to get some fresh air.

He donned a shoulder rig that housed the HK45 in an easy cross-draw position, slid the dagger back into its boot sheath, and then shrugged on the black duster.

When he stepped back into the kitchen, Silas asked, "Where the hell are you going?"

"Shopping," Asher replied.

CHAPTER 4

YOU COULD APPLY any number of derogatory adjectives to the back parking lot of the Pyramid Mall, but deserted was the one that came to Asher's mind as he parked the Jeep near the entrance of Paul's Guns & Sporting Goods. An autumn breeze scuttled dead leaves across the asphalt and they drifted quite a ways before finding a set of car tires to rest against. He glanced at the dashboard clock. 1:21 p.m. The lunch break shoppers had come and gone and it was too early for the evening rush.

As Asher entered the gun shop, he saw that he was not the only customer. A woman with thick, silken blonde hair cascading down to her shoulders stood at the pistol counter that ran along the left side of the store. Asher could only see the back of her head, but safe bet she was a looker. God wouldn't waste gorgeous hair like that on an ugly face.

A short, thin man wearing thick glasses that made his eyes look huge stood behind the chrome-trimmed glass counter, assisting the woman. Having never been to this particular shop, Asher presumed this was Paul. The guy looked more like a hellfire-and-brimstone Bible-thumper than a gun dealer.

He glanced up as Asher walked in. "Be with you in a few," he called out. "Feel free to look around."

Asher wandered the aisles, savoring the familiar scents of gunpowder and cleaning solvents as he surveyed the selection. Paul had an impressive stock, no doubt about it. Asher picked up a Mossberg twelve-gauge pump-action shotgun. A fine weapon for sporting and home defense, but not quite the type of tactical hardware he needed to replace the SPAS-12 that had been destroyed by the hitters currently enjoying an acid bath in his shower. Still, the Mossberg was a quality piece, its lines sleek and smooth with the lethal grace so inherent in firearms, and Asher took the time to enjoy the feel of it in his hands. He heard Paul talking to the blonde-haired woman but it was just background noise, no more intrusive than elevator music. He didn't pay much attention to it. Not at first anyway.

"Listen, ma'am," Paul was saying, "I'm not sure sellin' you a pistol is such a hot idea, and that's the pure and simple truth."

"Why not?"

That got Asher's attention. His head jerked up at the sound of the woman's voice. He hadn't heard that voice in over five years. Could it really be her? He still could only see the back of her head. "Larissa?" he said softly.

Her shoulders stiffened, then she slowly turned around and Asher saw the shocked look on her face. "Gabriel? Is that really you?"

Asher put the Mossberg back on the rack and

walked toward her. To his surprise, his heart was hammering. He and Larissa Peterson had been lovers before they each found someone else. He had gone on to marry Karen and Larissa had briefly dated one of his partners, a damn good operator named Malakai. Unfortunately, Malakai turned out to have some serious commitment issues and Larissa quickly broke it off. She ended up marrying Todd Auburn, another Company operative.

Asher studied her as he drew closer. She wore sunglasses so he couldn't see her eyes and there was a nasty scar on her left temple that had not been there the last time Asher had seen her, but otherwise she looked exactly like she had when they had been together. If only he could say the same; he was well aware that years of hunting men for a living had left its mark on him.

"Gabriel?" she said again.

"Yes, it's me," he said, emerging from the aisle of rifles. Her hands were stretched toward him in welcome and he reached for them.

A snarling mass of black and tan fur lunged at him. Asher jerked his hand back before the German Shepherd could tear it off at the wrist. He had not seen the dog when he first entered the store due to the configuration of the aisles; it must have been lying at Larissa's feet. As the Shepherd's teeth snapped shut, Asher nearly drew his gun and gave the dog a .45 caliber reprimand. But then he saw that the animal was wearing a guide harness. *A seeing-eye dog. But—*

Realization dawning, he looked at Larissa.

She bent down and stroked the Shepherd's head, ruffling him behind the ears. "Easy, Sirius. He's a friend. *Friend.*" She emphasized the word, but the way Sirius kept eyeballing him like he wanted to tear off a chunk or two made Asher unsure the dog was getting the message. Larissa stood back up and faced Asher. "Sorry. He's a bit overprotective."

"He's yours?"

"Sure is. Sirius is my eyes these days." She smiled. "I'm not wearing these sunglasses just to be fashionable."

"What happened?"

"I'll tell you all about it over lunch," Larissa said. "Just let me finish my business here and then we can go play catch up."

"All right." Asher's heart had stopped pounding, thank God. He didn't want to sit through lunch stammering like some idiot schoolboy on his first date.

Larissa turned back to Paul. "Sorry about that. He and I go way back and we haven't seen each other in a long time."

"Glad I could be around for the reunion." Paul sounded bored.

"Anyway," Larissa said, "you were about to explain to me why you feel I shouldn't own a handgun."

"Well, ma'am, it's like this—when Uncle Sam does his background check, they're gonna realize you got no business with a *pistola,* pure and simple."

"Because I'm blind?"

"Well...yeah."

"Why shouldn't a blind person own a pistol?"

"Uh, what for?"

"Protection, the same reason thousands of other people own handguns."

Paul sighed. "No offense, ma'am, but you might

shoot the wrong person. You can't see where you're aimin'."

Larissa started to say something, but Paul cut her off.

"Listen," he said, "this conversation is pointless anyway. They—the government—aren't gonna let you buy a handgun. It's that pure and simple."

"So 'they' don't need to know," Larissa said. "Is there anyone else in the store?"

"Just your friend there."

"Him I trust," Larissa said. "So let me put this in plain English for you. I live down in Albany and the only reason I took a bus all the way up here to your store is because I was led to believe that if I needed to obtain a handgun without going through the whole paperwork process, you were the man to see."

Paul abruptly looked more nervous than a priest caught masturbating. "Who told you that?" he demanded. "I oughta sue for slander." He tried to sound indignant, but Asher wasn't buying the act.

"A friend told me," Larissa replied. "That's all I can say."

Paul leaned forward, elbows on the counter. "Let me get this straight. You want me to sell you a pistol right here and now, without botherin' with the background check and all the red tape nonsense." His eyes flicked to Asher, then back to Larissa. "That's illegal, ma'am, pure and simple."

"I'm willing to pay extra."

"I see." Paul tossed Asher another glance.

"Your business, fella," said Asher. "Don't worry about me."

"You a cop?"

"Not even close."

"You have to tell me if I ask, you know."

"You asked and I told you. I'm not a cop."

Paul nodded, apparently convinced Asher wasn't a badge. "Okay, I have a few in the back that aren't on the books. Hold on a second." He disappeared through a doorway behind the counter and returned a few moments later with his illicit inventory. "Okay, not sure exactly what you're lookin' for, but I've got some Magnums here. A few three-fifty-sevens, a couple of forty-ones, and a handful of forty-fours."

"No Magnums," Larissa said. "Too much recoil. I want to protect myself, not break my wrist. Do you have anything in nine millimeter or forty cal? Something that will put a man down but without the kick of the Mags?"

Paul looked at her with newfound respect. "You know your guns, ma'am."

"My husband owned a lot of them."

Asher noticed she said *owned*. Past tense.

Paul pulled out a compact automatic. "This here's an Interarms Firestar." He ejected the magazine and then pulled back the slide to check the chamber, making sure the gun was unloaded. He popped the magazine back in and slid the weapon across the counter to Larissa. "Forty caliber semi-auto with a five-round clip and small enough to fit nicely in your purse."

Larissa felt around in front of her until her fingers found the pistol. She picked it up, testing the weight and balance. "Feels good," she said.

"It's a solid gun for close quarter self-defense," said Paul. "Which I assume is what you want it for."

"How much?"

Paul rattled off a price.

Larissa laid the gun down on the counter, then removed a roll of cash from her wallet and peeled off some fifties and twenties. Asher wondered how she could tell the different denominations, but then he spotted the small notches cut into the corner of each bill —two notches on the twenties, five notches on the fifties. Clever. She handed the money to Paul. "Here you go."

Paul tucked the bills into the cash register. The corner of his mouth quirked up and his tone was dry and amused as he said, "I trust you won't be needin' a receipt?"

Larissa slipped the Firestar into her purse. "No, but I could use a box of shells."

Paul grabbed a box of ammo from the shelf behind him and gave it to her. "Happy Halloween," he said. "On the house."

Larissa added the cartridges to her purse and then took a firm hold of the handle on Sirius' harness. The well-trained dog sprang to his feet, ready to guide his master. Larissa turned toward Asher. "I have one more errand to run inside the mall. Why don't you finish up whatever business you have here and then meet me at the restaurant? I think it's called Ruby's. I'm not sure since I haven't been up this way in a while."

"Yeah," Paul offered, "it's still called Ruby's."

"Sounds good," Asher said. "I'll meet you there in half an hour."

"It's a date."

Asher watched her leave the store, Sirius guiding her with remarkable ease through the maze of aisles and displays. He did his best not to let his eyes drop and check out how her backside looked in the pair of jeans, but he failed before she was halfway to the door. Damn good, that's how it looked.

He turned to Paul, who was looking at him with a smirk. Yeah, Paul knew where his eyes had been. Asher gave him a little grin. "Hey, can you blame me?"

"Not at all," Paul said.

"Appreciate you helping her out like that. She's an old friend."

"First Amendment gives folks the right to bear arms. Just doin' my part to uphold the Constitution, pure and simple."

Asher thought about telling him it was the Second Amendment, but decided not to bother. "So you're a patriot."

"You betcha. I bleed red, white, and blue, and never voted for a democrat in my life."

"I'm looking for a shotgun."

"I've got lots of shotguns." Paul gestured toward the aisle Asher had checked out earlier. "Browning, Mossberg, Remington—"

"Franchi," Asher interjected. "SPAS-12. Not the kind of toy you would have out on the floor. It's my understanding that you have some stock in the back that's not available to the general public."

"Who told you that?"

"A friend."

Paul rolled his eyes. "People and their friends. Everybody tells somebody else. It's a miracle the cops haven't busted me yet." He gave Asher a look that was probably meant to be hard, but the thick glasses totally ruined the effect. "SPAS-12 is gonna cost you a lot of money. Have you got a lot of money?"

"I've got the money."

"Then I've got the gun," Paul said. "Step into the back."

———

Twenty minutes later, Asher exited Paul's Guns & Sporting Goods with his newly-acquired SPAS-12 hidden under his duster. The gun had been used, but after field-stripping it and examining all the parts, Asher had been satisfied it was in working condition. He walked toward his Jeep to stash the shotgun before meeting Larissa.

The wind had kicked up a couple of notches, vigorous gusts blowing dead leaves around his ankles as he tucked the SPAS-12 under a heavy quilt in the back of the Jeep. Weapon concealed, his thoughts turned to Larissa, no doubt already seated and waiting for him at the restaurant. *Better fifteen minutes early than one minute late,* had always been one of her mottos.

He locked the Jeep and made his way through the mall to the restaurant, situated in the far corner of the food court. The hostess led him to where Larissa, just as he had expected, was already seated in a booth. Sirius lay quietly on the floor beside her, head resting on his paws, dark eyes watching Asher carefully as he approached.

He slid into the booth across from Larissa and almost instantly a waitress appeared to take their drink orders. Asher asked for a beer, Larissa opted for some white wine.

"So," Larissa said after the waitress departed, "how have you been, Gabriel?"

"Fine," he replied. Larissa still wore her shades and he could see his reflection in the dark lenses. "You?"

"I'm doing okay," Larissa said. "But God, it has been a while, hasn't it? Where did the time go? I honestly meant to stay in touch with you."

"Forget about it. After Karen died, I wasn't much fun to be around anyway."

"Are you much fun to be around now?" She grinned impishly.

He couldn't help but smile back, even though she couldn't see it. "Depends on your definition of fun."

"Are you still in the business?"

"You could say that."

"Still teamed up with Malakai?"

"No, we both went solo. Last I heard, he was working down in Miami."

The waitress returned with their drinks. As she set them down, Asher scanned the restaurant. The act was natural as breathing, something done subconsciously. When your enemies could be anywhere, it paid to always be on guard.

Here I am sitting across the table from a beautiful woman and the only thing I can think about is where the next bullet is coming from.

The thought was both amusing and tragic, a bittersweet commentary on the nature of his existence.

They placed their lunch orders—sirloin steak with mushrooms for Asher, chicken alfredo for Larissa—and the waitress departed once again. Asher leaned forward, clasped his hands together on the table, and looked at Larissa. Even with the sunglasses hiding her eyes, she looked stunning. "So," he said, "how are things with you and Todd?"

Her mouth twisted bitterly. "He's dead." Those two words held a lot of pain.

"God," Asher said. "I'm sorry. How—"

"Macklin got him."

The room suddenly felt ten degrees colder. "Macklin? You're sure?"

"Positive." Venom laced Larissa's voice. "I watched him kill Todd right in front of my eyes. Just gunned him down like a dog. I saw the scar on his throat just before he shot me in the head."

Asher glanced at the scar on her left temple.

"The bullet bounced off my skull—as you know, nine millimeter rounds do that sometimes—but the shock damaged my optic nerves, making me completely blind. The doctors say I'm lucky to be alive."

"They're right. Having a bullet ricochet off your head is pretty lucky." He grinned at her. "Then again, you always did have a hard head." Despite his attempt to lighten the mood, Asher was filled with anger. It was bad enough Black Talon tried to take him out this morning. But finding out that they murdered Larissa's husband and left her blinded? That really pissed him off.

"Lucky?" Larissa let out a hollow laugh. "I'm blind, Gabriel. Trapped in the dark for the rest of my life. How lucky is that?"

"Very lucky. By all rights, that bullet should have killed you."

She turned her head toward the wall, as if unwilling to face him. When she spoke, her voice barely broke above a whisper. "Some days I wish it had." She turned toward him again and reached for her wine.

That's when Asher saw the thin white scars criss-crossing her wrists.

She seemed to sense what he was looking at. "I tried to kill myself several times," she said.

"My God, Larissa." He didn't know what else to say.

She shrugged. "It was a rough patch. I had lost my husband and been blinded, all at the same time. Wasn't much of a stretch to think about checking out and once you start thinking about it, actually giving it a try becomes a whole lot easier." She smiled. "But I'm over it now. Grampy Cobby helped me through it. Remember him?"

"One does not forget Grampy Cobby," Asher said.

Matthew Cobb, a.k.a. "Grampy Cobby", was Larissa's grandfather, the man who had raised her when her parents died in a car wreck. Asher had met the man several times while dating Larissa, and while he was crotchety, foul-mouthed, and full of piss and vinegar, beneath his rough exterior beat a heart of gold. He was living proof that you should not judge a book by its cover, because once you got past first appearances, Cobb was one of the kindest, gentlest men Asher had ever met. No father and daughter had ever been closer than Larissa and her Grampy Cobby and it was easy to imagine his strong, wise hand guiding her through the tumultuous waters of grief and depression.

"Is he still around?" Asher asked.

"Lives about forty miles north of here, up in Dresden," Larissa replied. "He moved to Florida for about a year but came back when Todd died. He bought an old hunting lodge about two miles back in the woods and lives like a hermit now, off the grid. Says he likes the peace and quiet."

They small-talked their way through drinks and salads. Asher sensed they were both being careful to keep the conversation light, neither wanting to step on the other's emotional landmines. By the time their entrees arrived, he found himself fully relaxed and enjoying Larissa's company. When lunch ended, he would return to his world of blood and violence, but right now that world seemed far away. Right now he was not an assassin; he was just a man like any other, enjoying the company of a beautiful woman, having lunch with an old friend. It had been a long time since he felt this normal.

He had worked his way through half his steak before the conversation once again took a serious turn. "So," Larissa said, twirling her fettuccine with a fork, "are you seeing anyone these days?"

Asher shook his head, remembered she couldn't see it, and followed the headshake with, "No. After Karen, I just haven't had any interest in getting involved with someone again. Besides, it wouldn't be fair to the person I was with."

"What do you mean?"

"It's just..." Asher faltered, searching for the words; expressing his feelings had never been his strong suit. "I just don't think I could ever love someone else as much as I loved Karen," he finally said.

"Even after what she did to you?"

"Just because she cheated on me doesn't mean I stopped loving her."

"It must have changed things, though."

"Sure it did. But my feelings for her was not one of those things."

Larissa plucked a piece of alfredo-soaked chicken from her plate and gave it to Sirius. He took it carefully from her fingers, swallowed it whole, and licked his chops appreciatively.

Asher grinned. "That dog eats better than some humans."

"Sirius is my best friend," Larissa said, smiling warmly at the dog. "Have to take care of him." She took a sip of wine and set the glass back down on the table. "Gabriel, do you mind if I ask you a personal question?"

"Go ahead."

She fidgeted with her fork. "Have you ever wondered how things would have turned out if we had stayed together?"

Asher replied without hesitation. "Sure, I've thought about it, but it's impossible to know. Maybe things would have turned out better for both of us. Maybe they would have turned out worse. All we can do is play the hand we're dealt."

The corners of Larissa's mouth quirked upwards in a smile that could have been either amused or bitter; Asher couldn't tell which. "So you're saying you and I just weren't in the cards." She appeared to be looking straight at him, but of course that was impossible. Still, he could not shake the sensation that behind her dark glasses, her eyes were cutting right through him, probing for secrets. "Do you think you'll ever fall in love again?" she asked.

Asher thought it was a hell of a thing to ask. He'd agreed to lunch, not ripping open old scars. But he gave her an answer, though probably not the one she wanted to hear. "No. I don't think I'm capable of it anymore." He set his silverware down and pushed away his plate, the steak only half eaten.

Larissa fell silent, the easiness of their reunion bled dry by the specters of their past. Regrettable, but also inevitable. Yes, they had been friends once, but then they had become lovers, and Asher knew it was nearly impossible to go from the latter back to the former. Only fools dared try. Sooner or later the past will resurrect and the friendship will suffer at the cruel hands of love gone cold.

When Larissa spoke again, her voice trembled. "I loved you, Gabriel. Even when I was with Todd, I never stopped loving you."

"Larissa, don't do this."

"Let me finish. When we say goodbye in a few minutes, we'll probably never see each other again, so I want you to know the truth. And the truth is, I loved you. More than Malakai, more than Todd, more than anyone else. You were the only one I wanted to be with and it nearly killed me when you left me for Karen." A single tear slid out from under the glasses like a diamond emerging from darkness.

"I'm sorry," he said. "I loved you, but—"

Larissa waved him off. "Don't. Just...please...don't say it. I know you loved me in your own way, but there are two kinds of love: the forever kind and the fleeting kind. What you and I had was, at least for you, fleeting. Your love for Karen, that's the forever kind."

Asher had never felt so self-conscious. He would rather stand stark naked in Times Square on New Year's Eve than have this conversation. "What about you?" he asked. "Are you telling me you didn't love Todd?"

"Of course I loved him," Larissa replied. "But I only loved him because I could no longer love you."

Asher looked down at his hands, trying to compose a response, but he came up with nothing. His eyes focused on his ring finger. Even after five years, it felt bare without his wedding band. He looked back up at Larissa. "I'm not sure what you want me to say."

"I don't want you to say anything," she replied. "And I also don't want you to misunderstand me. I miss Todd. I really do. I would give anything to have him back. But he's gone and I have come to terms with that fact."

"You think I haven't come to terms with Karen's death?" Asher tried not to bristle, struggled to keep the thorns out of his voice.

"I think you're in love with a ghost," Larissa said softly, no doubt aware she was treading on sacred ground. "I think you need to let her go."

Asher felt something dark and dangerous trying to tear loose inside him. Even Sirius sensed it, abruptly lifting his head and firing off a low, throaty growl. "I think I need to say goodbye," Asher said, sliding from the booth.

She reached out her hand toward him. "Gabriel, don't...please...I'm sorry."

"Yeah," he said. "I'm sorry too." He tossed some money onto the table. "Lunch is on me. It was good to see you, Larissa. Take care of yourself." He turned and walked away. Some inner voice urged him to turn around, to go back and not let things end this way, but he ignored it.

"Gabriel!" Larissa called out. "Please..."

He could hear the pain in her voice.

He kept walking.

By the time Asher got back to his house twenty minutes later, his emotions had calmed somewhat, but his nerves remained on edge. He couldn't believe Larissa had said those things to him. Sure, they had been close once, but that didn't give her the right to just waltz back into his life all these years later and start saying shit like that.

He went inside to find Silas gone and plastic sheeting tacked up over the opening in the wall where his glass doors had been prior to their impromptu removal by autofire. Asher fished a beer out of the fridge and twisted off the cap as Mr. X emerged from the bathroom, a large burlap sack slung over his shoulder. Throw on a red suit and he would look like Santa Claus with a bag full of bones instead of toys. His watery eyes peered at Asher. "Silas left."

"Good." Asher tossed the beer cap in the trash can.

"Wants you to meet him down in the city tomorrow morning."

Asher nodded and took a drink. The cold beer felt great going down and went a long way toward soothing his nerves. Another six-pack or two and he might even regret not getting Larissa's number so he could call her up to apologize.

"I cleaned out your tub. Made sure none of the flesh had clogged your drain. Plugged the bullet holes in the wall and floor." Mr. X calmly rattled off the items as if they were a grocery list. "If you want new wallpaper or linoleum, that's your problem. The glass doors have to be ordered, so that's also out of my hands. The plastic will have to suffice for now. Anything else you think needs doing?"

"No."

Mr. X nodded. "Then I'll be leaving now." And just like that the strange little man vanished out the front door.

Asher finished his beer and then retired to his bedroom. A quick power-nap and then he would drive down to the city to meet with Frank and collect his fee for the Perelli hit. Silas had said tomorrow morning, but Asher didn't care. With any luck, by the time tomorrow morning rolled around, he would be back home with a little more coin in his coffers.

He placed the HK45 on the bed-stand within easy reach, then loaded the new SPAS-12 and leaned it against the wall. For one flickering moment, like a jump frame in a movie reel, he remembered how good it had felt to spend time with Larissa. For a few brief, stolen moments, he had been just an ordinary guy, not some cold-blooded killer who needed to have an arsenal within arm's reach just to catch a few minutes of shut-eye. But he was who he was. You could curse destiny if you wanted, but denying it was pointless.

Fully clothed, boots and all, he stretched out on the bed and closed his eyes against the afternoon sunlight spearing through the partially-shut blinds. Sleep came within minutes and in his final moment of consciousness, he wondered what he would dream about.

Nothing, as it turned out. Thank God for small mercies.

CHAPTER 5

ASHER AWOKE AN HOUR LATER. A glance at the clock told him it was 3:37 p.m. Perfect. By the time he reached NYC, the rush hour traffic would be thinned out, the madhouse of cars and trucks that clogged every road, street, and avenue finally clearing up. Every time Asher suffered through the crush of traffic on the city's highways, he was convinced he was trapped on one of Dante's infernal circles of Hell. He wondered what allure the city held for the honking, cursing, finger-giving fools in the vehicles clustered around him so tightly that the term "sardines in a can" seemed spacious by comparison. That anyone voluntarily chose to live in such a traffic-jammed hellhole boggled his mind.

Not that Frank Giadello lived in the actual city. Like so many of the wealthy and powerful before him, he owned a luxurious ten-acre beachside estate on Long Island, in the hamlet of Montauk. A ten-feet-high brick wall ringed the acreage to ensure privacy. There were only three ways to get a glimpse inside Frank Giadello's estate: by invitation, by air, or by climbing to the top of the Montauk Point Lighthouse three-quarters of a mile away and using high-powered binoculars. The only means of access was a large steel gate controlled from within a bulletproof shack manned twenty-four-seven by an armed sentry. Not your typical run of the mill security guards either, the kind that would fill their pants if someone so much as farted in their direction. No, Frank Giadello only employed serious operators.

One of those operators, a cold-eyed sentry with a face that looked chiseled from granite, gave Asher a steely once-over when he pulled up to the gate, then let him through. Asher navigated his Jeep up the drive, paying no attention to the lawn so manicured it made PGA golf courses look like rough-mown hay fields by comparison or the immaculately-clipped shrubs illuminated by soft, landscaped lighting. He had seen it all before.

The end of the driveway expanded into a large circle of pavement which served as a parking lot of sorts. In the center of this circle grew a rose garden, the flowers now gone, plucked by autumn's frozen fingers. Only bare, thorny branches remained, winding their serpentine way around a thick marble pillar erected in the midst of the roses. Atop this pillar perched a stone gargoyle and Asher imagined the creature's lifeless eyes glaring at him as he drove the Jeep around the circle and parked in front of the main entrance.

A wide stairway led up to the porch, which stretched across the entire front of the mansion, its roof supported by six marble columns that lent the place a Southern air. Asher took the steps two at a time.

At the front door, a guard greeted him, one he actually knew, a towering mass of rock hard muscle named Jean-Luc. He was dressed in black jeans and a windbreaker that did nothing to conceal his thick chest and bulging biceps. Asher had seen him in action and knew there was nobody better in a brawl. Blows that would knock most men senseless just bounced off Jean-Luc's six-foot-four frame like tennis balls thrown at a steel wall.

Asher gave him a nod. "How's it going, Jean-Luc?"

Jean-Luc had immigrated to New York from Quebec and still sported a Canadian accent. "Business as usual," he replied. "You here to see the boss?"

"Yeah."

"He expecting you?"

"He better be. He owes me money."

"Right. The Perelli job. Heard that went down smooth."

"It went down. Don't know about smooth." Asher's voice betrayed nothing, but in his mind he could hear the heartbroken sobs of a little girl and her widowed mother.

"Hold on a second." Jean-Luc turned to the intercom next to the front door and pressed a button.

There was an electronic buzz, followed by Frank Giadello's voice. "What is it?"

"Asher's here to see you, boss."

"Send him in." Frank's usually strong, authoritative voice sounded tinny and distorted through the small speaker.

As Asher stepped past him, Jean-Luc said, "Maybe I'll see you later. Been a while since we did a job together, eh?"

"That's because I prefer to work alone. Nothing personal."

Jean-Luc nodded. "Don't worry, no offense taken."

Asher headed down the hall toward Frank's office. Despite his preference for solo work, he had to admit that Jean-Luc was one of the few people he could stand, running a close second to his old partner, Malakai. He found the Canadian's constant cheerfulness and sense of humor refreshing. But Jean-Luc also knew how to be serious when the time came; that the only kind of cutting up that should be done on the killing field was the kind that involved a sharp blade and an enemy's throat.

To Asher's left, portraits of various Giadello family members adorned the walls, hung in perfectly symmetrical rows. Frank referred to it as the Wall of History and the last portrait on the wall was his. Asher had been regaled with the tale of Frank Giadello's rise to power so often that he sometimes felt as if he knew it better than his own life story.

Frank had inherited the shadowy empire from his father, Vinnie Giadello. Vinnie had sown the seeds that Frank would later reap, laying the groundwork, building contacts, establishing suppliers, all the things necessary for a successful illicit business venture. But while Vinnie's efforts garnered moderate success and wealth, it was not until Frank took the reins that the name Giadello became a force to be reckoned with in the NYC organized crime ranks.

Frank embraced the role of crime lord with near-religious zeal, his utter ruthlessness quickly rising to myth-like proportions as he climbed to the top through sheer balls and brutal bloodshed. He had carved his niche by outgunning his competitors and showing his enemies no mercy. Silas now commanded the day-to-day operations, but he was just a puppet. Frank remained the master, a puppeteer pulling the strings, making Silas and the rest of his criminal clan dance to his own cutthroat tune.

The hall ended at a set of solid oak double doors that led into Frank's office. Two more bodyguards bracketed either side of the entrance. Asher nodded at each of them as he approached. "Pierre," he greeted. "Andy." Pierre was Jean-Luc's brother and though the two bickered like cats and dogs, the animosity was a façade; in reality, the two were inseparable. Of the two brothers, Jean-Luc was the better gunman, but Pierre was the more dangerous, possessing a cruel, sadistic streak.

Andy Torlini was a newcomer, some wet behind the ears street punk that Frank had plucked out of the gutter. The kid was clearly too soft for this line of work. There was more to being a gunslinger than just packing heat. Andy was too eager to please, too eager to make his mark. Out on a strike, eagerness often led to mistakes, the kind of mistakes that got people killed. Asher had seen it happen all too often and hoped he wasn't along when Andy went out on his first job. He would rather lick a public toilet seat that hadn't been cleaned in three weeks than babysit a rookie.

Asher stepped past the two guards and into the inner sanctum of Frank Giadello. A large bulletproof bay window offered a view of a pair of cherry trees, the branches stark and skeletal in the moonlight beginning to seep through the clouds. Off in the distance, the lighthouse beacon could be seen sweeping the sky with metronomic regularity.

Frank sat behind a huge oak desk in front of the window. Two plush leather chairs were arranged in front of the desk, one of them occupied by Silas.

Frank gestured toward the remaining chair. "Have a seat, Asher." He then motioned toward the fully-stocked wet bar in the corner of the office. "Care for a drink?"

"I'll pass," Asher said as he sat down.

Frank wore a sharp, gray Italian suit that hung on him with the precise lines that only an expert tailor can provide. He leaned forward and folded his hands on the desk. His hands were flawless, professionally-manicured, and truth be told, looked rather feminine. But looks can be deceiving. Asher knew that Frank's hands, so soft and fragile in appearance, in reality were strong as iron and brutally unforgiving.

A few years ago, Asher had watched those hands literally beat a man to pulp. The victim had been identified as a traitor within the organization and Frank had used those manicured hands to relentlessly smash the man's body, again and again and again. The blows had rained down like the wrath of God until the traitor's face had been reduced to a mess of quivering jelly, horrible moans creaking from the bloody cavity of mangled lips and shattered teeth that had been the man's mouth. Only when the man no longer resembled a man—a slab of beef in a slaughterhouse looked more humanoid—had Frank wrapped his seemingly soft, weak hands around the traitor's neck and crushed the life out of him, cartilage crackling as the man's throat collapsed.

Frank buckled right down to business. "Asher, I have to tell you, nice work on the Perelli hit. You earned this." He flipped a plain white envelope across the desk as if dealing a card. It slid across the polished surface and into Asher's waiting hand. "It's all there."

Asher slipped the cash into his pocket. "Heard you had another job for me."

"You heard correctly," Frank said. "Tomorrow night I have a yacht bringing in a load of guns. My sources tell me the Perelli family is going to try to hijack the load when it reaches the marina. Naturally I'll have men on the yacht itself, but I want you at the marina, on the ground, running interference if anything goes down."

Asher wasn't sure he had heard right. "Did you say the Perelli family?"

Frank nodded. "You know how it is...you stomp on one snake, another one pops up to take his place. They're like damn weeds."

"So who's running the show now?"

"The wife. Rene Perelli."

"And she's making a play already? Have they even buried Perelli yet?"

"Just put him in the ground this morning."

Asher shook his head, recalling how Rene had cowered on the couch while he executed her husband. "Doesn't make sense. The Rene Perelli I saw does not have what it takes to pull a retaliation together this fast."

Silas joined the conversation. "Maybe you misjudged her. Or maybe watching her husband get snuffed helped her grow some balls."

Asher just ignored him.

"She wasn't even supposed to be home that night," Frank said. "That's why we didn't include her or the kid in the package. Had I known, I probably would have had you take her out too."

"And you know I wouldn't have been able to do that," said Asher.

Frank sighed. "Yeah, I know. You and your precious code."

The code.

Asher's code.

The Assassin's Prayer.

God, let not my bullet or blade shed the blood of innocents.

Karen had written that for him on the night he revealed to her that he was a Company assassin. He had been afraid that she would leave him, but she simply looked at him for a moment, then took out a piece of paper and wrote THE ASSASSIN'S PRAYER at the top. She had then penned the words of the prayer just beneath the title in her flowing, almost calligraphic script. She had presented it to him with uncharacteristic solemnity, then kissed him gently and told him that it did not matter, that she loved him no matter what he did for a living.

Tears stung Asher's eyes but he blinked them away. They'd be selling popsicles in Hell before he'd cry in front Frank or Silas. "You wouldn't understand," he said.

"You're right, I don't understand," said Frank. "Man, woman, child...anyone who gets in the way is fair game to be put down." He shrugged. "But it's no big deal. Let's see how this thing tomorrow night shakes out. If I decide Rene Perelli needs to be buried beside her husband, I'll have someone else do it."

"Speaking of tomorrow night," Asher said, "which marina are you using to offload the guns?"

"The one just down the road from your house."

"The Saint James Marina?"

Frank nodded. "You could walk to this job."

"Why so far away? Why not do the drop down here in the city? The way you have it set up now, you'll have to transport the guns over the road."

Silas answered. "Location. It's cow country, for God's sake. Nobody will ever suspect we're offloading an arms shipment there. And the marina is empty this time of year, so there's less possibility of unwelcome eyes observing the proceedings."

"And with you running interference on the ground," Frank added, "things should go smooth as silk."

"What time is it going down?"

"We expect the yacht—it's called the *Sea Shark*, by the way—to be there around midnight," Silas said. "You'll want to get there early to secure the grounds and take out any uninvited guests."

"Thanks for telling me how to do my job," Asher said sarcastically. "Are we done here?"

Frank nodded. "Yeah, that's it. I'll have one of the guest rooms made up for you."

Asher stood up. "I'm not staying."

Silas stood as well. "You're actually going to drive back home *tonight*? You just got here."

"All I came for was my money and my next job. I got both, so there's no reason for me to stay."

"You spend too much time alone, Gabriel. It's not healthy. Stay here among friends for a while."

"You're not my friend."

"Only because you won't let me be."

"And whose fault is that?"

Frank slapped his desk to get their attention. "All right," he said, "that's enough bickering for one night, kids. Asher, if you don't want friendship, that's perfectly okay with me. The only bond that needs to be between us is my cash and your guns. Love, loyalty, friendship...all as overrated as ribbed condoms. So have a safe trip home."

Asher turned and walked out of the room. He heard Frank say something, probably *adios* or *sayonara* or some stupid crap like that, but he didn't respond. He just pulled open the double oak doors, exited past Pierre and Andy without acknowledging them, and strode briskly down the hall until he reached the front door.

As he stepped out into the darkness of early night, Jean-Luc no longer manned the front door, so Asher found himself alone at last. Only then did he let the tension bleed from his body. Silas was so zealous in his quest to repair their broken friendship that it blinded him to the fact that his attempts only served to anger Asher. Forgive the betrayal? Not a chance in hell.

But as Asher walked down the steps to his Jeep, he acknowledged that sometimes he felt a sense of loss, an empty ache for a fallen friendship. The feelings never lasted long—just a flickering second or two—but Asher could not deny their existence.

The emotional tug-of-war scraped his nerves raw as he fished his keys from his pocket. The hollow pain made for a long drive home.

CHAPTER 6

THE NEXT NIGHT, Asher arrived at the St. James Marina at precisely 2200 hours. The mercenary team showed up 60 minutes later.

Approximately 200 meters northeast of the marina, in a large field of waist-high wild grass, squatted a crumbling heap of blackened rubble and scorched stone that had once been a luxurious riverfront mansion before it burned to the ground forty years ago. From the shadows of these old ruins, Asher watched the mercenaries through night-vision binoculars that stripped the world of color, leaving behind only varying shades of gray, black, and green.

The four men arrived in a dark van with blacked-out windows. Asher pegged them as mercs by their tactical clothing, disciplined precision of movement, and TDI Vector submachine guns threaded with suppressors.

Asher wondered why Rene Perelli had contracted outside talent for this job. Peter Perelli had been a powerful up-and-comer in the organized crime ranks and his execution could not have crushed the entire organization. Sure, Asher had inflicted some damage, made them suffer some losses, but there still should have been enough goons left to rally to Rene Perelli's cause and carry out this attempted hijack of the Giadello arms shipment.

Then again, most organized crime triggermen know how to conduct a hard strike about as well as a vegan knows the best way to cook veal, so maybe that was why Rene Perelli had opted for professionals.

And there was no doubt that the four-man team that exited the van decked out in black from boots to caps were pros. They moved with the lethal grace inherent to men who are at home in kill-zones. With quick, stealthy movements, they melted into the shadows, merged with the darkness, and took up positions in a pine grove near the water's edge. They had chosen their concealment well; the entire merc team would be invisible to the *Sea Shark* when it motored into the marina.

The St. James Marina was little more than a cement launching ramp for small boats and several wooden docks that stretched from the shore out into the deeper waters of the Hudson River to allow the occasional yacht to moor. As long as he had lived in the area, Asher had never seen the place manned. A dilapidated trailer served as a main office, but it looked like its better days had been somewhere around the time of bell bottoms and disco balls. No lights glowed in the windows. Asher and the mercs had the place to themselves.

Targets identified, Asher lowered the binoculars and glanced up at the dark, dense sky. Thick clouds suffocated the stars and marginalized the moon. The mercs had to be loving this weather. It was a perfect night for a hijacking.

Well, except for the death dealer lurking in the darkness, about to put bullets in all of them.

Asher reached for his weapon of choice for tonight's mission: an Israeli-made Galil Sniping Rifle. The GSR featured a folding stock, making it one of the most compact sniping systems on the market, more of an accurized assault rifle than a true sniping rifle. But this was not a surgical strike where millimeters mattered. With the GSR, Asher could put five shots into a two-inch circle at 200 yards, plenty accurate for this job. After all, the hijackers' heads were a lot bigger than two inches.

Asher flipped down the integrated bipod and adjusted the legs, stabilizing the Galil. A 6x40mm scope was mounted on the receiver. He looked through it, feeling the rubber eyepiece press against his skin. The scope was a light-gathering model, capable of utilizing all latent light, including moonlight and starlight, and magnifying it to such a degree that the shooter could see the target even in the dark.

Asher swung the rifle onto each of the four merce-naries, marking their positions. When the time came to put bullets downrange, he would have only seconds to take down quadruple targets. Knowing where they were and how far apart they were spaced would be crucial to his success.

He tracked left to right, then right to left, and then repeated the sequence several more times, getting a feel for how far he would have to swing the GSR before acquiring sight picture on his multiple targets. He didn't worry about anyone hearing the shots; the rifle sported a sound suppressor that doubled as a muzzle brake and flash suppressant. Whatever killing went down here tonight would go down quietly.

Through the scope, the mercs looked restless. They repeatedly checked their chronometers, then scanned the river. They appeared keyed up, ready to go, ready for action. Just sitting around was probably playing hell with their nerves. One merc fired up a cigarette, match flaring brightly. It was the first sign of poor discipline anyone on the team had exhibited.

From the way the others kept glancing at him, Asher pegged the smoker as the leader. A few meters to his left was a black man with a rubbery-looking scar on his upper lip. The other two were your standard issue white boys, completely nondescript.

Asher decided to take the leader first. Basic combat axiom—destroy the head honcho and the followers often fall into confusion, and confusion leads to vulnerability. Asher hoped the sight of their commander falling would freeze the others long enough for him to drop them as well.

He mentally crunched the numbers. It would be close. He had to be quick and smooth on the trigger. The margin for error was razor thin.

Lights appeared off to Asher's left where the river first curled into view and a few moments later the rumble of engines reached his ears as the yacht eased toward the marina docks. Asher didn't bother confirming that it was the *Sea Shark*; just the way the mercenaries tensed up and shifted into action stances told him it was show time.

Asher drew a bead on the merc leader. Through the scope, he saw the man drop his cigarette, crush it under his boot heel, then exhale his last drag in a cloud of smoke. Asher aligned his crosshairs, applied 2.5 pounds of pressure to the fine-tuned trigger, and sent his first 7.62mm bullet right through that gray haze. The merc leader staggered backward, his entire oral cavity—teeth, tongue, and soft palate—blown out the exit wound in the back of his neck.

Asher barely registered the kill. He was already swinging the GSR onto his second target, the black merc.

Trigger pull. Recoil. Impact.

The scar on the man's lip vanished, erased by a bullet. A large chunk of his head vanished as well.

Moving with the fluid precision of a well-oiled war machine, Asher tracked right, seeking target acquisition on the third merc. The man's startled face filled the scope and Asher blew it off. Four seconds elapsed, three men down.

The last merc tried to take evasive action, but he was just a split second too late. As he spun to his right, seeking cover behind the nearest tree, Asher drilled a bullet through his ribs and into his heart. The guy pitched sideways, dead before he hit the dirt.

Asher took a deep breath and exhaled, releasing the tension and adrenalin that had built up during the six seconds it took him to terminate the merc team. His breath plumed like dragon-smoke in the cool night air. He stowed the GSR back into its case, then extracted himself from the area. His work here was done.

He was home in time to catch the second half of *The Late Show.*

CHAPTER 7

LATER THAT NIGHT, Asher awoke to the sound of his cell phone ringing. He glanced at the alarm clock, red numbers glowing in the dark. 2:30 a.m. Safe to assume it was not the Christian Children's Fund calling to ask him to sponsor a starving kid.

He answered on the fourth ring.

Before he could even say hello, Frank Giadello bellowed in his ear as if someone had twisted his scrotum into a Gordian knot. "They hit us! Ambushed the van, whacked my guys, and took my guns!"

Asher reached over, turned on the light, and cracked his bedroom window open a couple of inches. He listened to the deep, throaty croak of bullfrogs in the marsh across the road.

"Asher? Are you there?"

"Yeah."

"Did you hear what I said?"

"Yeah."

"Well, say something, for God's sake."

"Something." Being rudely awakened in the middle of the night brought out the best in him.

"What I don't need right now," Frank growled, "is a smartass."

"Sorry," Asher said, but he didn't even try to sound sorry.

"Yeah, I'm sorry too," Frank said, and he didn't sound like he meant it either. "Sorry to tell you that I need you down here by dawn. Got it?"

"Yeah."

———

Asher didn't make it by dawn—he caught a couple hours of shuteye instead of jumping right in his Jeep— but he did arrive at the Giadello estate by midmorning.

Jean-Luc met him out front and escorted him around back to the Olympic size inground pool. A portable massage table had been erected on the patio and Frank was being rubbed down by two scantily-clad blondes—Missy and Michelle, if Asher recalled correctly—who giggled like schoolgirls as they slopped massage oil all over Frank's neck, shoulder, back, and legs. Jean-Luc went over to a small table which had been laid out with a continental breakfast, grabbed a bagel, and departed the vicinity.

Asher poured himself a glass of orange juice from an ice-chilled carafe. Sunrays needled deceptively hot against his skin; the calendar might have said October, but the onset of Indian summer made it feel more like June. Moist and muggy were the meteorological catch-words of the day.

Asher sat down at the breakfast table and sipped on

his juice while Missy and Michelle gave Frank the kind of massage that did not miss a single nook or cranny. They had enough empty space between their ears to float a zeppelin, but God had compensated them for that deficiency by blessing them with gorgeous bodies and gifted fingers.

Frank turned his head and pretended to see Asher for the first time, though he had little doubt the crime boss had known he was sitting there all along. Frank Giadello didn't miss much. "Asher," Frank said. "Good to see you again." He jerked his thumb over his shoulder at the girls. "Want to take one for a spin? They'll do anything." He winked. "And I do mean anything. I've done things to these two that would make a porn star blush and they haven't batted an eye."

"I'll pass. But thanks for the mental image."

"Your loss." Frank swung his legs off the table and looked at the girls. "Excuse us, ladies, but Mr. Asher and I have some private business to discuss, so I need you to disappear for a while."

Missy and Michelle's ripe, ruby lips turned down in fake, sultry pouts but they obeyed like good little pets, leaving Frank and Asher alone on the patio.

Frank donned a white terrycloth robe and then sat down at the table across from Asher. He picked up a croissant and took a bite. "So," he said between chews, "about our little disaster last night. Somebody ambushed the van, slaughtered my guys, and made off with the guns."

"Think Rene Perelli hired two teams?"

"Conjecture at this point, but it seems to be the likely answer," Frank said. "Probably the team you took out was just a decoy. I bet Perelli never intended to hit the yacht. I bet her plan all along was to hit the van."

"Looks like she's got brains to go with her beauty."

"Yeah, well, I want those brains blown out the back of her pretty little head," Frank growled. "This is a war I don't need right now."

"If you're asking me to put her down, you've got the wrong guy."

"I haven't asked you anything yet."

Silas chose that moment to return, coming out onto the patio through the sliding glass doors that led into the main house. His rubber-soled shoes squeaked as he walked across the wooden deck.

Frank asked, "What is it, Silas?"

"Someone here to see you. Says he's here on Rene Perelli's behalf and he'll only talk to you."

Frank popped the last piece of croissant into his mouth and chewed it slowly, thoughtfully, as if the act of mastication would give him the wisdom to know what to do with this unexpected turn of events. "All right," he said at last, "bring him in and let's hear what he has to say."

"You got it." Silas turned and walked away.

Frank poured himself a glass of orange juice and looked across the table at Asher. "You armed?"

"Of course."

"Good. Whoever this guy is, he's not leaving here alive."

"Thought you wanted Rene Perelli."

"Her messenger will do for now."

Silas returned with the stranger in tow and Asher gave him the once-over. Crew-cut hair atop a rugged, angular face with dark, hawk-like eyes and a nose that had been broken more than once. Thin lips curved with cruel arrogance. Linebacker shoulders over a narrow waist and arms crisscrossed with scars, mostly old, some fairly recent. Yeah, this guy had gone a few rounds with the Reaper. Probably one of the mercs behind last night's ambush, if Asher had to guess.

Frank gave no indication of what he thought of the man. He simply gestured toward the carafe of orange juice. "Care for a drink?"

The stranger glanced at Asher, sizing him up with a piercing gaze, then looked back at Frank. "I'll pass. This isn't a social visit. I have a message from Rene Perelli."

"And you are?"

"Jack Robbins."

"I've heard of you," Asher said. "You're a merc. Supposedly one of the best. And one of the most expensive."

Robbins smiled, but it lacked humor. Looked more like a death's head rictus. "You get what you pay for."

Frank tapped his finger against the side of his glass. "Did Rene Perelli pay you enough to have your guts carved out with a spoon? Because that's what's about to happen to you."

Robbins' smile stayed pasted in place. "No, it's not."

"You sure about that?"

"Actually, yeah, I am."

"And what makes you so sure?"

"There's a sniper in the lighthouse. Right now, he's watching us the crosshairs. Anything happens to me, he puts a bullet in you."

Frank glanced at the lighthouse in the distance, just visible over the top of his privacy wall. "That's three-quarters of a mile away."

"My guy can shoot the nuts off a gnat from a mile out. Your nuts are presumably much larger and therefore easier to hit."

"What if I don't believe you?" Frank snapped. Being challenged put him in a foul mood, so right now an alligator with a cattle prod rammed up its ass was probably friendlier than Frank Giadello.

Robbins held up his right hand and mimicked pulling a trigger with his index finger.

A few seconds later the carafe of orange juice exploded from the impact of the sniper's bullet.

To his credit, Frank never even flinched. But his eyes smoldered with anger.

Robbins lowered his hand. "Satisfied?"

Frank spoke to Asher while keeping his enraged eyes fixed on Robbins. "Asher, what do you think?"

Asher shrugged. "I think you probably want to rethink that whole carving his guts out with a spoon idea."

"You also want to pay attention," Robbins said. "Because if we're done with all the blowhard bullshit, all I came here to do was give you a message. Once I've delivered that message and heard your answer, I'll be on my way and the crosshairs will be off your dick. There really is no need for all this hostility."

"No need for hostility?" Frank snarled. "Are you kidding me? You killed my men, stole my guns, walked into my home, put a bullet in my breakfast, and then have the audacity to tell me there's no need for hostility? Who the hell do you think you are?"

"I'm a mercenary," Robbins replied. "And this is just business. I was hired to take down your van, hijack the guns, and deliver a message to you in person. So that's what I did and that's what I'm doing. Nothing personal or hostile about it. It's just a job."

Frank glared across the table at Robbins, tapping the side of his glass, then sighed in exasperation and growled, "Fine, let's hear the message."

"Perelli says you can have the guns back...for three hundred thousand. Says it can't replace the husband you took from her, but it's a start."

Asher did some quick mental math. The arms shipment had been both large quantity and high quality, military surplus stolen from a base up near the Canadian border, with a street value somewhere around half a million. Rene Perelli was allowing Frank some latitude, permitting him to still turn a profit, but teaching him a tough lesson at the same time. Looked like she had made a smooth, rapid transition from whimpering widow to cunning crime queen.

Frank looked like he had just been sodomized sans lube. "She wants me to buy back my own guns? Is she out of her damn mind? Tell her she can kiss my ass. If I want my merchandise back, I'll *take* it back, not buy it. I'll bury her next to her dead husband before I pay her a single dime."

"I'll convey your message to Ms. Perelli."

"You do that. Silas, get this scumbag son of a bitch out of my sight."

Asher watched as Silas escorted the mercenary away and then turned to Frank. "Thought he wasn't leaving here alive."

"That was before his sniper aimed a bullet at my balls," Frank said. "Nothing like a little testicular harassment to make you adjust your plans."

"So what's the plan now?"

"I want you to follow him and the first chance you get, take him out. But before you do, I want you to find out where my guns are. Got it?"

Asher rose to his feet. "Yeah, I got it." He sighed inwardly. Time to get more blood on his hands.

———————

The late morning traffic on the Long Island Expressway was a total nightmare. Trying to tail Robbins' nondescript gray Chevy Blazer in the tangled bumper-to-bumper mess of taillights, exhaust smoke, and angry horns put Asher's skills to the test. Finally, the vehicular congestion thinned out. He stayed back about a quarter-mile, just barely keeping the Blazer in sight, letting cars pass and fill in the gap between him and Robbins. Now all he had to do was sit back, set the cruise, and wait for the mercenary to make a pit stop. There was no sign of the mystery sniper.

Three hours later, Asher was starting to think that Robbins possessed the world's biggest bladder as the merc passed one rest area after another with no indication of stopping. Asher's own bladder begged for relief.

Finally, traveling I-87 between Poughkeepsie and Albany, Robbins pulled off into a rest area. "About time," Asher muttered following the Blazer. He swung the Jeep into a spot at the opposite end of the parking lot and gave Robbins a sixty second head start before making his way inside.

The men's bathroom was down a short corridor past the vending machines. As Asher approached the door, a man came out, nearly colliding with him. Asher's muscles tensed, but the guy wasn't Robbins, just some traveler finished taking a leak.

"Whoa! Sorry about that," the stranger said. "Guess I need to slow down." He smiled and nodded an apology.

Asher gave a slight nod back. "No problem."

When the man was gone, Asher drew his sound-suppressed .45 from beneath his duster and went through the door in a rush. Robbins was a professional and Asher's best chance of success was to catch him off guard, not saunter in like he was out for a Sunday stroll.

Robbins was washing his hands at the sink. The merc's head jerked up at Asher's sudden intrusion. Recognition instantly flared in his eyes and he went for his gun. He was fast, but not fast enough. Before he even cleared leather, Asher rammed the HK into his stomach. "Take your hand away from your gun," he said.

Robbins hesitated, calculating the odds, running the numbers in his mind. In a reversed situation, Asher would have done the same thing. It took Robbins less than three seconds to realize any play was suicide. He let his hand drop to his side.

"Good boy," Asher said. "Now let's go into one of the stalls and have a little chat. Keep your hands where I can see them." He backed Robbins into the nearest stall, maintaining constant pressure with the HK45. Given even a razor-thin sliver of a chance, Robbins would make a play that could turn things into a real clusterfuck.

"So what's the plan?" Robbins asked once they were in the stall and Asher had secured the door. "Blow my brains out and flush them down the crapper?"

"The only thing I want in the crapper is your gun. Take it out—slowly—and toss it in."

Robbins took out his gun, an expensive Kimber Stainless Pro Raptor, and dropped it in the toilet. Water splashed as the gun sank to the bottom of the porcelain bowl.

Robbins' eyes burned with hot coals of hate. "Do you have any idea how much that gun cost?"

"Pretty sure you can afford another one with what Perelli is paying you."

"Don't play me for a fool. You have no intention of letting me walk out of here alive."

"Why don't you just have a seat and we'll see how it goes."

"You've got the gun, so right now you're the boss." Robbins reached behind him to lower the seat.

"Leave it up." Forcing Robbins to sit on the toilet without the benefit of the seat would keep the mercenary's center of gravity lower, making it more difficult for Robbins to launch himself into some kind of half-assed heroic play.

Robbins obeyed, but Asher caught the foxlike cunning in the man's eyes. Robbins might be a cool-cat mercenary, but he would never cut it at the poker table. His eyes gave up too much information. Robbins' intent to try some sort of counterattack was as obvious as a neon sign glowing in the dead of night. Asher knew he could not afford to let down his guard.

Neither could he afford to spend much time on this interrogation. This was a fairly remote stretch of I-87, but it was still a public rest area and it would only be a short time before somebody came in to use the facilities. Asher had to rip the answers out of Robbins fast.

"Listen," he said to the mercenary. "I'm going to skip the foreplay and get right down to the dirty stuff. I want you to tell me where you took Frank Giadello's guns."

"What you want really doesn't mean jack to me, because you've forgotten one very important piece of information."

"And what would that be?"

Robbins smiled nastily. "I'm not alone." His eyes shifted to the stall door.

Asher reacted instantly. He dropped to the floor a fraction of a second before autofire knocked on the door. The bullets blew through and punched into the wall just above Robbins' head. Dust and debris exploded into the air.

Asher hit the ground and rolled onto his back with the kind of snake-strike speed that comes from a whole lot of years spent in the killing game. He saw a pair of rubber-soled boots under the stall door and wasted no time putting a bullet in the gunman's ankle. The guy yelled in pain and toppled to the floor, landing with a hard thud on his left shoulder.

Asher took one nanosecond to register the man's face. It was the stranger who had almost bumped into him outside the bathroom. Another nanosecond and Asher knew he was engaged in a firefight with the mystery sniper, who still clutched the Micro-Uzi he had used to spray the stall door. One more nanosecond and Asher realized this rest area had been a prearranged rendezvous point.

And then there were no more nanoseconds to spare. There was only survival. The sniper lifted the Micro-Uzi back into play. Robbins lurched off the toilet. Asher was pinned down flat on his back with a threat in front and a threat behind.

Robbins might get his gun out of the toilet in another second or two, but the sniper had his gun out right now. That made the sniper the primary threat.

Asher canceled that threat by hammering a .45 slug right between the sniper's eyes and out the back of his skull. The Micro-Uzi tumbled from lifeless fingers as chunks of bone and brains splattered the far wall.

One down, one to go.

Asher immediately turned his attention to Robbins. The merc had his Kimber out, dripping with water, and nearly had it leveled at Asher's head.

No time to use his gun. Asher kicked Robbins in the left kneecap. The merc's body jerked and buckled from the crippling blow. Robbins managed to pull the trigger, but he was off balance. The bullet banged off the tile a couple inches from Asher's face.

Asher tried to get his own gun into play, but the narrow confines of the stall made it tough to maneuver. As he thrust the HK toward Robbins, the merc chopped down with the Kimber, pistol-whipping the .45 right out of Asher's hand. It bounced off the rim of the toilet and skidded under the divider into the next stall.

Asher didn't waste time going after it. Prostrate and gun-less, he faced an enemy who was upright and armed. If he wanted to survive the next few seconds, he needed to bring Robbins down to his level.

So he reached up, grabbed a handful of Robbins' balls, and yanked down viciously. The merc snarled in pain and involuntarily hunched lower in an auto-response attempt to ease the agony and avoid having his nuts torn off. As he did so, Asher delivered a hard jackrabbit kick against the inside of the mercenary's injured left knee. Between the ball-yank and the knee-kick, Robbins dropped to the floor.

As Robbins crumpled, Asher used his free hand to chop the merc's wrist, numbing nerves and sending the Kimber tumbling. His other hand continued to crush Robbins' gonads.

The merc managed to extricate himself from Asher's clutches, but Asher was pretty sure it cost him at least one torn testicle. Both men scrambled to their knees and proceeded to trade punches, the blows short and sharp due to the close-quarter confines of the stall. Asher knew this would not be a long, drawn out battle. This was going to be a quick, nasty, down-and-dirty slugfest that would be over in less than a minute with one of them shaking hands with the devil at the gates of Hell.

Asher took a punch to the kidney. Returned the favor with a blow to Robbins' solar plexus. Ducked the right elbow strike the merc whipped at his temple, then got caught by a left cross that clipped his chin. The blow didn't really daze him, but he feigned injury and prayed to the gods of war that the mercenary took the bait.

Robbins swallowed it hook, line, and sinker.

Believing Asher to be vulnerable, the merc tried to seize the moment by spearing a set of stiff fingers at his enemy's seemingly exposed throat. Had they struck, they would have snap-crackle-crunched the assassin's Adam's apple and left him choking on splinters of cartilage. But Asher dodged the throat-jab, causing Robbins to miss his intended target. This left Robbins slightly off balance, his arm overextended. Asher grabbed the merc's wrist with one hand, keeping the arm extended, and delivered a sharp, powerful blow with the heel of his other hand to Robbins' elbow. The merc's arm broke like a piece of balsa wood, bone shards bulging in grotesque knots just beneath the surface of the skin.

Still on his knees, Asher spun around behind Robbins, grabbed him by the back of the neck, and slammed his head down against the front edge of the toilet bowl. A large chunk of the bowl shattered and broke away, leaving behind a grin-shaped gap full of jagged porcelain teeth. The water sluiced out, soaking both men.

The blow to the head would have knocked out an average man, but Robbins wasn't average. While clearly dazed from having his skull used as a battering ram, he still managed to dig out a combat knife from wherever it had been hidden. With Asher still grasping the back of his neck, Robbins couldn't turn his head to line up a target, so he just jabbed backward blindly.

Asher dodged to the side without relinquishing his grip, narrowly avoiding being stabbed. He then drove Robbins' head back down into the broken toilet. The jagged porcelain stumps smashed into the merc's face and acted like saw blades, shearing through gums and palate and cutting open the corners of the mouth so that Robbins' upper jaw and lower jaw were on opposite sides of the broken rim. The classic curb-stomp position.

Asher climbed to his feet and stood over Robbins. In the movies, this was the climactic moment when the hero would spout off a witty one-liner before dispatching the villain. But this was not the movies and Asher knew he was no hero. So instead of wasting time coming up with a smartass comment, he just raised his boot and stomped down as hard as he could on the back of Robbins' neck. The sharp porcelain stalagmites finished ripping through flesh and bone so that the merc's body slumped to the floor, his lower jaw still attached. The upper jaw and the rest of his head tumbled into the empty toilet, splattering it with blood.

Asher stood there for a moment, staring down at the gruesome sight as the combat adrenaline cooled in his veins, then reached down and retrieved his HK45 before exiting the stall. He stepped over the corpse of the sniper, the punctured head haloed in crimson. He left the bodies—as well as the Kimber and the Micro-Uzi—where they lay. This being a public spot, there was no chance for clean-up and sanitization. The next traveler who stopped to use the facilities was in for a shock. Public restrooms are notoriously filthy places, but nobody expects to find a bisected head staring up at then from the bottom of the bowl.

Outside in the parking lot, Asher let his brain poke and prod at the problem he now faced. He had survived his rumble with Robbins, but killing the merc had also killed his chance to find out where Frank's hijacked guns were holed up. There was no question he could have forced Robbins to spill his secrets. Crank a couple bullets into the kneecaps, maybe blast one into the balls, and the mercenary would have been begging for mercy. But that was no longer an option.

Asher walked across the parking lot to Robbins' Blazer and peered inside. Stuck to the windshield by a suction cup mount was a GPS. Could he be that lucky?

He tried the door, but it was locked. The keys were no doubt on Robbins' corpse, but Asher didn't have time to retrieve them. Instead, he smashed open the driver's side window with the butt of his gun. Messier than a key, but just as effective. He reached in and plucked the GPS from its holder.

He didn't waste time studying it right there, but instead hopped into the Jeep and high-tailed it back toward the city. He stopped at the next rest area and used the GPS's touchscreen to access the information he was looking for. Before his violent demise in the dirty stall of a remote public bathroom, Robbins had programmed in his destination, an address in the downtown slums of Albany.

Asher was willing to bet that's where Frank's hijacked guns were.

———

It was mid-afternoon by the time Asher got back to the Giadello estate. The return trip had seemed longer than it actually was because he could not stop thinking about how wretched Robbins had looked lying on the floor, head sheared in half, blood splattered everywhere. Talk about a rough way to check out.

Robbins had been just like him, a modern day gunslinger, and Asher couldn't shake the chilling sensation that he had looked into the mirror of his own fate. It was like the hand of God had reached down, grabbed him by the scruff of the neck, and rubbed his face in his own sickening future. *See that? That's how your life is going to end. Someday you'll be on the wrong end of a gun and it will be sayonara, sucker.*

The thought was more depressing than a country-western song.

Frank no longer lounged poolside when Asher returned. Andy, nauseatingly fresh-faced and eager-to-please, escorted Asher to the office where Frank was shooting billiards with Silas. Asher heard the sharp crack of hard, resinous balls smacking into one another as he walked in, followed by a muffled thump as one dropped into a pocket. Other balls caromed off the cushions.

Frank studied the lay of the table before glancing at Asher. "Is it done?"

"Yeah, it's done."

Frank chalked up his cue stick. "Did you get the information?"

"Best I can tell, Robbins rented a little rat hole in Albany for him and his team. Some place called Arbor Apartments. I pulled the address off his GPS. I'm betting the rest of Robbins' team is there, sitting on your guns."

Frank lined up a shot and smoothly stroked the cue stick, driving the cue ball across the green felt. The target ball slid down the cushion and plunked into the corner pocket. Frank reached for the chalk again.

"Take some of the boys," he said, "and go get my guns. And be sure to make an example out of Robbins' men so that Rene Perelli will know she can't mess with me and get away with it. She needs to realize that every move she makes against me will have serious consequences. Understand?"

"Yeah," Asher said, "I understand. But you're forgetting something."

"Such as?"

"Compensation. You're barking orders but I'm not one of your bitch-boys. I'm a freelance contractor and I expect ten grand per target. I'm guessing this merc team is somewhere around five men. Maybe less, maybe more, but I'd bet on it being in that ballpark. Since I already took out Robbins and the sniper, I expect—"

"You killed the sniper?" Frank interrupted.

"Gave him a forty-five caliber lobotomy. Which means I expect there to be at least three more mercs at the apartment."

"I thought this might come up." Frank leaned his cue stick against the table, went to his desk, and took a thick envelope from the drawer. He walked back over and tossed it on the pool table. It landed next to the eight-ball. "There should be fifty grand in there. That'll cover the ten for Robbins, the ten for the sniper, and thirty for the rest of them. If it turns out there's more than three at the apartment, I'll settle up after."

Asher picked up the envelope. It was heavy, stuffed with cash. He counted out ten thousand and laid it down on the table before pocketing the rest. "I don't want any money for Robbins," he said as something dark twisted through him. "That one's on the house." He saw Frank looking at him quizzically but didn't explain any further. Didn't know if he could explain it even if he wanted to.

He turned and left the room.

CHAPTER 8

WHAT A SHITHOLE.

That was Asher's first thought as Andy found a parking spot across the street from Arbor Apartments. The four-story building had definitely seen better days. At least half the windows were broken. Asher wondered what had shattered them, rocks or bullets. In this part of town, could have been either.

Asher felt the cargo van settle as Andy shifted into park and killed the engine. In the passenger seat, Silas turned and looked at Asher, who was sitting directly behind Andy. "So what's the plan?"

"Just sit tight for a few," Asher said. "I want to get a feel for the place before we go in." He knew it was possible that the merc team had gotten nervous and jack-rabbited for parts unknown when Robbins failed to return. They were pros, and pros possessed that sixth sense that warns them when a deal has gone south and it's time to vacate the vicinity.

As Asher studied the street, Pierre and Jean-Luc fidgeted in the seats next to him like ADHD-afflicted toddlers. The two brothers hated sitting still, especially when there was a job to be done. Asher knew he would have to keep a close eye on Pierre. Bloodlust burned in the man's eyes and Asher had no intention of letting him go on a rampage. If the psychotic SOB wanted to go kill-crazy, he could do it on his own time.

It was 8:30 at night, but not even the darkness could hide the reeking desolation and desperation of Arbor Apartments. Under harsh streetlights, the grass grew high enough to hide a Buick and weeds rioted in the crumbling foundation. This was not a neighborhood; this was a wasteland of fast food wrappers, old newspapers, and empty beer bottles, a diorama of dereliction strewn with the detritus of lives gone sour. Whores, crack-heads, gangbangers ... these were the broken souls that called this sewer of suffering home.

As if to reinforce the point, a pack of youths—a motley crew of blacks, Hispanics, and white boys, not one of them over sixteen—perched on the fissured concrete steps leading up to the entrance of the building, a boom box blaring rap music at ear-bleed decibels. The bass-heavy beats slapped at the van with sonic backhands.

Asher turned away from the window and looked at his team, a term he used loosely. Between Andy the rookie and Pierre the psycho, Asher felt like a damn babysitter. Maybe he should have packed formula and diaper rash ointment instead of bullets and extra mags. He was reminded once again of why he preferred to work alone.

"All right, listen up," he said. "The target is apartment 4D. We go in hard but use suppressors. Andy, once we're inside, you stay in the hall and cover our six."

Andy looked disappointed. "Come on, man, I want to—"

"I don't care what you want," Asher snapped. "Just shut up and do what you're told. Got it?"

"Yeah." Andy pouted sullenly. "I got it."

Asher reached for the door handle. "Let's go."

Outside the vehicle, the rap music overpowered all other sounds. Asher yearned to put a bullet through the boom box, but he refrained from drawing his gun as he led his team across the street, watched with hostile eyes by the gang. As he started up the steps, the youths closed ranks, standing shoulder to shoulder all the way across, forming a solid wall of human, hoodie-wearing flesh.

Whichever of them spoke first would be the leader. Asher's money was on the tallest guy in the middle of the human wall. Black, with a shaved head, mirrored shades, and gold chains around his neck that looked fake enough to have come from a Cracker Jacks box. What didn't look fake was the butt of the Smith & Wesson .357 jutting from the front of his baggy jeans. Stupid place to carry a pistol, unless you wanted to accidentally blow your balls off.

"Who da fuck you be?" Tall Guy asked. He didn't look a day older than fifteen, but the tone of his voice was surprisingly mature, despite his gutter vocabulary.

"Doesn't matter who I am." Asher raised his voice to be heard over the music. "How do you want to play this? Should we whip out our dicks, see whose is bigger? Or maybe just go to guns right here in the street." He paused before offering a third option. "Or maybe we can be civilized about this and you can just tell me what I need to do to get inside."

Asher couldn't see Tall Guy's eyes behind the reflective shades, but he felt himself being sized up. Tall Guy apparently took his measure and then a gold-capped grin sprouted on the gangster's face. "You's got balls, white boy. Gots ta give ya cred fo' dat. Question is, do ya gots two g's?"

"Maybe," Asher said. "What's it buy me?"

The smile broadened. Tall Guy was clearly enjoying the game, looking to all the world like a cat playing with a mouse, completely unaware that he was really a mouse pestering a very dangerous cat. "For two g's, I won't turn this music down."

"That music sucks, so why wouldn't I want you to turn it down?"

"Because if I turn it down, the boys you come to kill in apartment 4D will know you be here to smoke 'em."

"So they paid you to keep an eye out for us. You turn down the music, it's the signal that we're here."

"Bingo, boy-o."

"How much they pay you?"

"One thousand."

"And if I give you two?"

"Two g's on top of one g would be cause for great celebration, and everyone know dat celebrations require lots of loud tuneage."

"Your crew helps load the cargo we came for and you've got a deal."

"Screw dat noise. We ain't yo' slaves."

"Slaves worked for free. I'm offering you two grand."

"Good point." Tall Guy pondered for a moment, then said, "Okay, pass me da bread and we gots a deal."

Asher nodded. "Silas, pay the man." He could have paid the guy himself, but he was pretty sure if he flashed an envelope stuffed with $40,000, the gang-bangers would no longer be satisfied with a paltry $2,000.

Sure enough, when Silas pulled a roll of cash out of his pocket, Tall Guy asked, "How much you's got dere?"

Silas didn't bother trying to lie. "Five grand."

Tall Guy held out his hand. His shiny smile never wavered. "Give it to me."

Silas looked at Asher, who gave him a slight nod. Now was not the time to quibble over a sudden price hike.

As Tall Guy pocketed the payoff, Asher asked, "We good?" He phrased it in the form of a question but put a hard edge on his tone to make it clear that it was really a statement.

Tall Guy signaled his street soldiers to step aside and waved Asher and his team up the stairs with a flourish. "Good to go, my brutha. Enjoy your killing game. We'll be right here, crankin' up da soundtrack to da apocalypse."

"You're a regular Samaritan," Asher said as he led his team up the rundown stairs to the front entrance of the apartment building. The music blasted unabated at their backs.

The heavy wooden door bore the scars of the ghetto, graffiti scrawled across nearly every inch of space. Nothing unusual, just the typical vulgarities and insults. F-bombs and "Eat My Dick" seemed pretty popular and apparently some girl dubbed "Betty Big Boobs" was available for a good time if you called 555-796-BLOW.

Given the neighborhood, Asher expected the door to be locked, but it opened easily when he turned the handle. Inside was a sparsely-furnished lobby containing a couple of battered chairs, an equally-battered coffee table, and a few dying plants with brown, brittle, dusty leaves.

Asher led the way up. The stairway stank of rotting garbage, urine, and stale sweat. Asher had to give it to Rene Perelli—she had picked a hell of a place to hide the guns. If Robbins' GPS hadn't yielded up the address, they never would have located the hijacked shipment. Once they had the address, it had been as simple as calling the landlord and finding out which apartment had been most recently rented.

They reached the fourth floor and stepped out into the hallway where the air wasn't exactly fresh, but damn near heaven compared to the filthy stench of the stairway.

"Everyone make sure you're locked and loaded," Asher said. He didn't doubt they were, but he had not lived this long by taking anything for granted. Making an assumption might mean you caught a bullet in your ass. So he checked his gun and while the others checked theirs. Satisfied that all magazines were properly seated and all chambers stuffed with a round, he gave the order. "Let's get this done."

He led the way down the hall. Apartment 4D was the first one on the right, the number-letter combination barely readable through the grime and graffiti covering the door.

"Should we knock?" Jean-Luc grinned, keeping his voice low.

"Absolutely." Asher fired a powerful kick just below the knob. Wood splintered and the door flew open. They stormed into a squalid room that reeked of cigarettes, booze, and unwashed bodies.

The three mercenaries sat on the couch watching a rabbit-eared black and white TV with the classic exploding arrow scene from *Rambo II* playing on the screen. At the sudden intrusion, the three men leapt up and grabbed for their guns. They were pros and they were fast, but not fast enough. Asher killed the first one with a .45 slug to the center of the chest. He saw a second one pitch sideways, a hole ripped in his ribcage and heart by a bullet from Silas' gun.

The last merc almost made it to the Micro-Uzi lying on the coffee table in front of him, but before he could actually pick up the weapon, Asher pumped a round through his palm. The mercenary flopped back against the sofa, clutching his mangled hand, jaw clenched in pain.

Asher pointed his pistol at the sweet spot just above the merc's upper lip. "Got a name?"

The mercenary glowered at him but answered. "Rodriguez."

On his peripheral, Asher saw Pierre prowling restlessly around the room, kicking aside the takeout containers and food scraps littering the floor. Several roaches that looked big enough to give Godzilla a run for his money crawled out of a pizza box and scuttled out of sight beneath the TV stand.

"What do you *cabrons* want?" Rodriguez demanded. "Who the hell are you?"

Asher shifted the HK slightly and fired once, the sound muffled by the suppressor.

Rodriguez' good hand flew up to cover his bullet-split ear. Blood oozed between his fingers.

"Let's get one thing straight," Asher said. "I ask the questions, not you." He stepped forward and rested one boot on the coffee table. He leaned his right forearm on his raised knee, keeping the .45 aimed at the soldier of fortune whose fortune currently seemed to have gone belly up. "Now, tell me where the guns are."

"How about I tell you to go hump a dead *burro* instead?"

The shot came out of nowhere, so unexpected that Asher thought he had accidentally pulled the trigger. Rodriguez' head snapped back as a bullet blew his brains out in wet chunks onto the wall behind him.

Asher spun around and saw smoke curling from the muzzle of Pierre's Glock. "What the hell do you think you're doing?"

Pierre slid the Glock into a shoulder holster beneath his jacket. "I was tired of you having all the fun," he said. "Besides, the guns are in the back bedroom. I already checked."

Asher walked over until he and Pierre stood just inches apart. He still gripped the .45, tempted to blow the cool, smug look off Pierre's face and do the world a favor. "You ever pull shit like that again, I'll put two in your guts and crack a beer while I watch you die hard and slow. You got that?"

Pierre's expression never changed. "Sure," he said. "Sorry, Gabe." He didn't look sorry one bit.

Asher turned to Silas and Jean-Luc. "Someone go tell those street rats to get these guns loaded."

"I'll do it." Jean Luc exited the room.

"Speaking of those street rats," Silas said, "what are you planning to do about them?"

"What do you mean?" Asher asked.

"They're witnesses."

"They're kids."

"They're gangbangers."

"They're still kids," Asher said. "We're not gunning down a bunch of kids."

"Your call."

"Damn straight it is."

They left the corpses lying in the filth of the apartment, food for the cockroaches, and joined Andy out in the hall. Asher could taste blood and gun smoke in his mouth and wished for a shot of whisky to wash it away. "Any problems?" he asked.

"No," Andy replied. "Well, nothing to be worried about anyway."

"That's for me to judge. What happened?"

"The neighbor in 4C," Andy answered. "I heard a dog growl once, then this hot little honey sticks her head out and asks if there was something wrong, because she thought she heard some strange noises."

"She say what kind of noises?"

"Yeah, she said it sounded like someone coughing."

Shit! She heard the shots. It was impossible to completely silence a gun. Even through a suppressor, a shot made a significant coughing noise. But few people, hearing that cough, would be able to identify the source.

Asher looked at Andy. "What'd you say?"

"Told her we were visiting a sick friend who has

lung cancer, which would explain the coughing she heard."

"That's pretty lame. She buy it?"

"Seemed to. She even apologized for bothering me." Andy looked at Pierre and winked. "Trust me, she was definitely not a bother. Prime, grade-A woman, I'm telling you."

Pierre looked amused. "Maybe I'll come back tomorrow and see if she wants to go out on a date."

Asher said, "Pull your brain out of your dick and let's get out of here before I give you a forty-five caliber castration just for the fun of it."

Pierre grinned. "You'll need a bigger gun."

Jean-Luc returned with the street gang in tow. They filed into the apartment like a string of worker ants and emerged carrying crates of stolen firepower which they lugged down the stairs and into the back of the van.

Asher's nerves were scraped raw by the time they got back on the highway. He leaned his head back against the rest and thought about the three mercs they had left behind in the apartment, dead meat for the rats and roaches. They had lived by the gun and they had died by the gun. It forced him to consider his own mortality. How long before it was his turn to dance with death?

Asher pushed the thought from his mind as Andy flipped to a classic rock station and "Dirty Deeds Done Dirt Cheap" blasted from the speakers. After having his ears violated by the street punks' gangsta rap, AC/DC was a welcome relief. The van rattled with rock and roll thunder as they headed back to the Giadello estate.

CHAPTER 9

ASHER and his team arrived back at the Giadello estate a little after midnight. Pierre, Jean-Luc, and Andy disappeared in search of late-night snacks, alcohol, sleep, nocturnal companionship, or all of the above. Asher and Silas reported to Frank's office.

Silas quickly relayed the events of the evening. Frank listened, features expressionless, until Silas finished his report. He then stood up, walked out from behind the desk, and without warning slapped Silas across the face. The vicious crack of flesh striking flesh filled the room. It was a savage blow, a real head-knocker, but Silas didn't even flinch. He took the insult without wincing, eyes staring straight ahead as a red welt blossomed on his cheek.

"Are you a fool?" Frank demanded. Without waiting for an answer, he strolled over to the bar and mixed himself a screwdriver. For a few moments, the only sounds in the room were the clink of ice cubes and the gurgle of vodka and orange juice being added to the glass.

Frank took his drink over to his desk and sat down. His gaze latched onto Silas like a tiger selecting his prey. "Answer me, Silas. Are you a fool?"

The palm-print on Silas' cheek glowed a fiery red. "No, I'm not a fool," he said. "Why do you keep asking me that?"

"Because only a fool would be stupid enough to leave a witness alive."

Asher cut into the conversation. "I made that decision." He felt strange coming to Silas' defense, but Frank was tearing into his underling for decisions Asher had made. He didn't care if Silas took a beating, but not on his behalf. "I called the shots. The witnesses were a bunch of gutter rats. I'm not going to gun down a bunch of kids just because they were born in a bad part of town."

"What about the woman?"

"She didn't see anything. No reason to kill her."

Frank's eyes pierced Asher like fishhooks, digging out the truth. "I know what's really going on here. This is about you and your code. You won't kill a woman."

"I won't kill an innocent," Asher said. "Man *or* woman."

"But you've got a soft spot for women," Frank countered. "You have ever since your wife checked herself out of the game."

You bastard. Hearing Karen's suicide so casually and callously referenced boiled Asher's blood. He wanted to launch himself across the desk at Frank, but it was a reactionary, lizard-brain impulse that he easily controlled.

Frank shook his head. "You're a slave to the past, Gabriel. Your wife scribbles some mumbo-jumbo shit on a napkin one night and you act like it's the greatest discovery since the Dead Sea scrolls."

Asher refused to debate the issue. What Frank called shit, Asher called sacred. Frank could beg, plead, cajole, bribe, threaten, or whatever, but Asher would not willingly shed innocent blood. To him, there was no greater evil.

Frank said, "All right, I won't ask you to violate your precious code, but this woman is a loose end that I need tied up for my own peace of mind." He looked at Silas. "Take Pierre, go back to the apartment, and eliminate her."

Asher's conscience crawled. Could he actually sit back and do nothing while an innocent woman fell under the gun? Yes, he decided, he could. Because he would not be the one pulling the trigger. Semantics, sure, but it let him walk out of Frank's office feeling that he had stayed true to his code. Yeah, the woman would die...but not by his bullet. He could live with that. At least, that's what he tried to tell himself.

Outside, the night air was muggier than it had any right to be this late in the season. A faint breeze tried to ease the humidity but only managed to send a few dead leaves scuttling across the driveway where they came to rest against the stone wall encircling the rose garden.

Asher leaned against one of the porch columns and watched Silas and Pierre roll down the driveway, taillights glowing in the dark, off to complete their murderous assignment. The woman would be dead before the morning news. She might even be dead in time to *make* the morning news.

Weariness seeped into Asher's bones. Maybe it was time to put this life of blood and death behind him. Just hang up his guns, pour himself a big ol' glass of Jack Daniels, draw a bath so hot it was just shy of boiling, and try to soak away a lifetime of sins.

His mental imagery smash-cut to Karen, her lifeless body lying in a tub full of crimsoned water. She hadn't exactly been innocent—she broke his heart and betrayed him in the worst possible way—but she had not deserved to die, not even by her own hand.

Overhead, the stars seemed to stare down at him like accusing eyes. He pushed away from the pillar, climbed into his Jeep, and headed for home.

He had just crossed the Tappan Zee Bridge when he realized he wasn't really heading home.

Not yet, anyway.

CHAPTER 10

LARISSA PETERSON WAS one of those early to bed, early to rise kind of people. Head on the pillow by 9:00 p.m., awake by 5:00 a.m. Which explained why she was finished washing her breakfast dishes by 5:45 a.m. Not that it took long to wash dishes for one person and it had been a long time since she shared breakfast with anyone. Of course, part of that was her own fault; after Todd's death, she had erected invisible walls around herself and hung up a sign that said THIS HEART NOT OPEN FOR BUSINESS.

But even with her prickly defenses in place, there should have been men hitting on her, asking her out, if only in attempts at one-night stands. But it almost never happened. It was her blindness, she knew. Men acted as if it was some sort of communicable disease like leprosy rather than a mere handicap.

She didn't waste her days pining for a man. Yes, she got lonely sometimes, but she had Sirius, and the German Shepherd showed far more loyalty than any man she had ever known except Todd. Sirius took her wherever she wanted to go, would give his life to defend her, and never made false promises just to get her into bed. With a friend like that, who needed a man?

She dried her hands on a threadbare towel and smiled to herself. Who was she trying to kid? Despite everything Sirius gave her, there were other things the dog could never offer. She would never hear the words "I love you" from Sirius' lips (though he let her know in countless other ways). Sirius couldn't wrap his body around her in the dark and hold her close, whisper sweet nothings into her ear. Nor could he make hot, passionate love to her.

Larissa felt no shame at craving sex. Sometimes she considered going to the nearest bar and picking someone up. No names, no numbers, no commitments... just raw lust, somebody to touch her, caress her skin, kiss every inch of her naked body. But while she felt no shame in her desire, she knew she would never yield to the temptation. Sure, there might be fleeting pleasure in a few hours of unemotional sexuality, but what she really missed was lovemaking. To her, sex and love were inextricable. She just couldn't see giving herself to a stranger.

She threw the towel into a drawer by the sink, then went into the living room, winding her way through the few articles of furniture she owned without hitting a single thing, the path etched into her brain through years of repetition. When she first rented the apartment, she had constantly barked her shins, but those days were long gone. Like a lot of other things in her life. Things like her eyesight and husband, for instance.

She heard the rustle of fur as Sirius moved out of her way. Whenever she worked in the kitchen, he liked to lie in the doorway between that room and the living room. It was his way of protecting her, of keeping himself between her and the door, through which untold dangers could enter, and she loved him for his thoughtfulness.

She sat down on the sofa, purchased for a pittance from the local thrift shop, careful to avoid the butt-poking spring jutting through a tear in the fabric. Her multiple attempts to cram the offending coil back down into the sofa's innards had thus far failed and she couldn't afford to buy a new one, especially now that she had spent most of her savings buying a pistol. The insurance money she had received after Todd's death had been far less than she had expected and the majority of it had been devoured by hospital bills as expensive surgeons tried in vain to restore her vision, taken from her by a madman named Macklin.

No longer able to afford the mortgage on the dream house she and Todd had bought in Virginia, Larissa migrated north to Albany and found this dirt-cheap apartment in the slums. Yes, it was in a not-so-nice part of town, but for some reason her neighbors left her alone. Being blind, she couldn't bother them, so they didn't bother her. Sure, she heard the occasional wolf-whistle or lewd remark when she walked down the street, horny teenage punks playing it cool in front of their friends, but no one ever molested her with Sirius by her side, and her apartment was the only one in the building that had not been burglarized. Maybe the hoodlums only left her alone out of pity, but whatever the reason, she had somehow managed to eke out a semblance of peace and independence here.

Of course, she didn't want to live here forever. But

employment opportunities for a blind woman were scarce and those that were available didn't pay much. She had landed a job answering phones at a health club for slightly more than minimum wage plus mediocre benefits and as long as she stayed where she was, she could survive on that. But as for leaving town and seeking a better life? Forget it.

She found the TV remote and clicked on the early morning news. Though she would never again see the images on the screen, Larissa still "watched" television. It made her feel normal, part of everyday society; as long as she could hear the dialogue, her imagination could supply the pictures. Not the life she had wished for, but it was the life she had learned to accept. Unconsciously, she rubbed the thin, white scars on her wrists.

Sirius suddenly growled, a low, rumbling sound that raised the hairs on the back of Larissa's neck. She fumbled with the remote and managed to mash down the MUTE button. She listened carefully, but didn't hear anything, which surprised her. Her hearing had grown more acute after the loss of her sight, one sense compensating for the absence of another, a phenomenon she had heard about but never really believed until experiencing it firsthand.

"What is it, boy?" she asked, turning her head toward the German Shepherd. "Did you hear something?"

When Sirius didn't respond, Larissa turned the TV back on. Sometimes the dog was *too* possessive, growling if so much as a roach scuttled across the floor. Like last night, when she heard those coughing noises in 4D, the adjacent apartment. Sirius had growled his fool head off until she had been compelled to open the door and ask the man in the hall what was going on. She had listened to his story of a friend with lung cancer and then withdrawn back into her apartment, telling Sirius to hush. The guy had not been a very good liar, but she really didn't care. Whatever was going on next door was none of her business.

In this part of the city there were more devils than angels and you learned how to live and let live if you wanted to survive.

She shifted on the couch, trying to find a more comfortable position while also trying to avoid an unwelcome probe by the exposed spring. She tried to concentrate on the news, but her mind didn't want to focus on the latest round of saber-rattling from North Korea or the price of oil or the endless unrest in the Middle East.

No, the only thing she wanted to think about was Asher.

She kept reliving their disastrous lunch date, a sorrowful blooper reel playing on an endless loop in her head. God, she had been such a fool. She had spent the last five years unable to forget him and then when she finally found him again, she promptly ripped open old wounds.

Way to go, stupid, she chided herself. Meeting him again had left her shaken. Up until that moment, she had not been fully aware of just how deep her feelings for him ran. And to have him walk away from her so easily cut her to the core.

Sirius growled again and then the growl erupted into a full-blown snarl. Larissa heard a crash as someone kicked in her door. Fear raced through her and she instantly thought of the pistol she had purchased. It was in her bedroom, lying on the night stand. It might as well have been on the moon.

She heard that coughing sound again. This close, she recognized it for what it was—suppressed gunshots. Sirius yelped and Larissa's heart turned to ice.

"Sirius!" she cried, leaping to her feet, forgetting about the coffee table in front of her. The edge bit into her shins. She stumbled and fell, scattering knickknacks everywhere as she slid to the floor. The worn carpeting scraped against her palms like sandpaper. Footsteps came toward her. She opened her mouth to scream for help, but a rough voice cut her off.

"Scream and you're dead. Not easy dead, either. *Hard* dead. I think you know the difference."

Larissa bit back the cry. "Who are you?" She tried to keep the fear out of her voice but failed miserably. "What do you want?"

"My name is Pierre." A heavy French-Canadian accent thickened his voice. "I am here to kill you."

He said it with disconcerting pleasantry. Larissa imagined a smile on his face, as if he had said nothing more menacing than, *Would you like to buy a vacuum cleaner?* Terror twisted her guts into nauseous knots. There was no way out. Pierre stood between her and the door. Blind and unarmed, she was completely at his mercy. Right about now all she could do was pray.

Her mind raced, searching for something to say, keep him talking, delay the inevitable. "What did you do to my dog?" she asked.

"Check for yourself. He's about four feet to your right."

Larissa crawled across the floor until her hands felt familiar fur. "Sirius?" she whispered, clinging to a faint shred of hope. But the dog didn't stir. "Sirius?" Then her hands slid into the bloody ruin of the dog's breast and her hope turned to ashes. Tears stung her blinded eyes. Sirius would never again guide her steps or lick her face. He had died defending her.

Grief and loneliness and fear ripped at her as she cradled the dog's head in her lap. She scratched him behind his furry ears the way he liked, half-expecting his back leg to go spastic in response, thumping the floor with pleasure the way it always did. But of course, that would never happen again. "No," she moaned, rocking back and forth. "God, no, please."

Rough fingers closed around her upper arm like a steel band. Sirius' head fell from her lap and hit the floor with a hollow *thunk* as Pierre dragged her to her feet. "Save the tears," he growled as he hauled her across the room. "They won't work."

Numb with grief and stricken with terror, Larissa didn't even struggle, unaware of where Pierre was dragging her until he flung her onto the bed. She rolled onto her back, bedsprings creaking harshly, and horror pierced through her grief, bubbling up within her like black, ugly oil. Pierre not only intended to kill her, he intended to have some fun first. The thought was unbearable. *Please God don't let this happen to me!* She began to kick and claw.

Something hard and cold thudded against the bridge of her nose. "Hold still," Pierre snapped.

Larissa froze, realizing he had the gun to her head. "Please don't do this to me," she pleaded.

"Shut up," Pierre growled. "I didn't come here to listen to you yap. Next time you open your mouth, I'm going to put something in it."

Go ahead. I'll bite it off and spit it in your face.

Under the threat of the gun, Larissa didn't struggle as Pierre bound her wrists and ankles to the bed posts with paracord that bit deep into her flesh. It hurt so much she thought the bone itself must be bruising.

Pierre tightened the final knot and then Larissa heard the whisper of steel on leather as he drew a knife from a sheath. Terror and shame burned through her as he cut away her clothes. She choked back a sob every time the blade grazed her skin, an icy kiss laced with wicked portent. She could hear Pierre chuckling softly, the sound of pure evil. She didn't know how she was going to be able to stand what was about to happen to her.

He touched her then, places he had no right to touch. Her skin crawled and she started to sob. She prayed for numbness, for a way to detach herself from reality until this hell ended, but it was useless. She felt his every slimy touch, the rough groping of her body, the sour smell of his breath, the cheap scent of his cologne. She laid still and suffered, tears streaming down her cheeks.

But when she felt his weight crush down on her, felt him position himself for the final violation, she could not hold back the horrific cry that escaped her lips.

"*No, please!*"

———

Asher arrived at the Arbor Apartments and wondered if he was too late. The early morning traffic around

Albany had been a snarled mess of congestion that had shaved precious minutes from the clock.

The sun was just coming up as he walked down the rough, weed-sprouting sidewalk. The rays caromed off cracked concrete and crumbling bricks, bleaching the color from the urban scenery as Asher entered the apartment building.

He found Silas in the lobby, leaning against the wall at the foot of the stairs. Pierre was nowhere in sight, presumably already upstairs taking care of business.

Silas looked at him in surprise. "What the hell are you doing here?"

Without breaking stride, Asher fired a right cross that Silas never saw coming. The blow struck him flush on the jaw, whipped his head around, and sent him slithering to the floor in a crumpled heap of unconsciousness.

Asher bounded up the stairs to the fourth floor and made his way to apartment 4C. He reached inside his duster and wrapped his fingers around the butt of his HK45 when he saw a blood-puddle seeping out from under the door.

Damn it!

He was too late. The woman was dead.

He drew the HK with his right hand and nudged the door with his left. It opened at his touch, revealing torn hinges and a splintered jamb. The coppery scent of blood rushed out at him, the bitter taint biting into the back of his throat.

But it wasn't the woman's blood like he had expected. He looked down at the blown-open carcass of a German Shepherd. The glassy eyes seemed to stare up at him with a mute plea. Asher saw a glint of metal through the mess of blood. It was the dog's tag and even through the gore, he could read the name.

SIRIUS.

Asher felt something dark and cold touch the edges of his heart. Then he heard the desperate cry from the back of the apartment.

"No, please!"

Asher rushed toward the sound of Larissa's voice. Emotions wrenched at him, screamed through his veins, set his blood on fire.

The bedroom door hung half-open. Through the gap, he saw Larissa bound, naked, and spread-eagled with Pierre positioned on top of her. Asher felt his control snap as rage sliced through him like a million hot razors. The air swirled red before his eyes.

He kicked open the door. Pierre's head jerked toward the violent intrusion. "What the—" Then he saw the .45 in Asher's fist. "Hold on, wait a second, man, you don't want—"

Asher cut loose with the HK and bullets tore into Pierre's throat. Whatever he'd been about to say vanished in a spray of scarlet froth. The impact hammered him off the bed and onto the floor. Blood spattered onto Larissa's face and chest, the crimson shockingly bright against her pale skin.

Asher's heart pounded with fury and vengeance. He stormed over to where Pierre writhed and gurgled on the floor and emptied the magazine point-blank into his skull, blowing it to pieces.

When his rage finally ebbed, Asher realized he was still pulling the trigger on an empty gun, his mind locked in a deadly rhythm of retribution. Shock rushed in to replace the rage. What the hell had happened to him? He stared down at the shattered remnants of Pierre's head and wondered how he had lost control so badly. His killing had always been cold, methodical, dispassionate—he had controlled *it*, not vice-versa. But even as his mind asked why, his heart knew the answer, even if it was an answer he did not want to face.

As he slid the .45 back into its holster, Larissa called out, "Who's there?"

The fear in her voice made Asher want to bring Pierre back from the dead just so he could kill him all over again. He said, "It's me, Larissa."

"Gabriel?"

"Yeah." Asher plucked the dagger from its boot sheath, cut through the paracord binding her to the bed, and gathered her into his arms. She clung to him desperately, sobbing into the crook of his neck. He just held her and let her cry.

After a few moments, she lifted her head and brushed the tears from her face. "Sorry," she said quietly. "I just...you know..."

"You've got nothing to be sorry for," said Asher. The wetness in her unfocused eyes made them gleam like emeralds, but they were emeralds set in raw, red sockets. More raw redness glowed angrily on her ankles and wrists where the cords had scraped her skin. He let her go and rose to his feet. "We have to get out of here. The people I work for want you dead."

He was having a hard time wrapping his head around the fact that just days after once again crossing paths with Larissa, he now found her living next door to his latest targets and marked for death by Frank Giadello, his client. What were the odds? With that kind of luck, he should go buy a lottery ticket.

Maybe it's not luck, some inner voice suggested. *Maybe it's fate.*

He mentally shut that shit down. No time for those kinds of thoughts right now. He needed to focus.

He ejected the spent magazine, popped a full clip into the .45, and jacked a round into the chamber. Now he was ready to rock 'n' roll again if need be.

"They want me dead?" Larissa echoed. "Why?" Without waiting for an answer, she slid from the bed and groped toward the dresser.

Asher knew he shouldn't look but her body drew his eyes like metal to a magnet. The sight of her nakedness made him realize how long it had been since he had known a woman's touch. Not since Karen's death. He felt a twist of pain, the memories like a nest of thorns in his heart. He watched Larissa dress, sleek muscles moving under her silken skin, and remembered a time that seemed so long ago and yet like only yesterday.

Larissa suddenly paused. "Are you watching me?"

"No," Asher said a little too quickly.

Larissa canted her head in his direction. "I don't believe you."

"Believe me or don't," Asher replied. "But we have to go. Now."

Larissa faced him for another heartbeat and Asher saw the emotions in her blinded eyes. Then she turned away and continued dressing. She retrieved her Firestar .40 pistol, tucked it into her waistband, and let her shirt fall over it. "Okay," she said. "I'm ready."

"Let's get out of here." But before they could go anywhere, Asher heard the creak of the front door being pushed open. The HK45 in his fist, he took up position in the bedroom doorway where he was partly shielded but still had a clear view of the living room and front entrance. His finger tightened on the trigger, taking up the slack.

The door swung open all the way, but nobody appeared in the entrance. Asher waited as adrenaline thundered in his veins. He could hear the sound of Larissa's breathing right behind him.

Then Silas called to him from out in the hallway. "You in there, Gabriel? What the hell, man? You damn near broke my jaw."

"I'll put a bullet in it next time if that's what it takes," Asher said. "Stand down, Silas. One way or the other, we're walking out of here."

"I can't do that, Gabe, and you know it. She's a target."

A target. How many times have I used that term myself? Asher thought. Using the word "target" dehumanized the victim and made it easier to drop the hammer. But Larissa was not just some random target, she was someone Asher had once cared for, and they would be selling popsicles in hell before he stood by and let her die.

"She's an innocent, Silas. You know that."

"Doesn't matter." Silas sounded hard and grim. "Step aside, Gabriel. Don't make me take you down. What's she to you anyway?"

Asher sensed Larissa close behind him. He remembered their lunch date a few days ago, her confession that she had never stopped loving him. He couldn't return that love but at least he could keep her alive. His mouth twisted at the irony—he refused to love her, but he would kill for her.

"She's my friend," Asher replied. "But I guess that doesn't mean anything to someone like you."

"Go to hell, Gabe. That's got nothing to do with this. My orders are to eliminate the bitch and that's what I intend to do. So either get out of the way or let's get this dance over with."

And just like that, the time for talking was over.

Asher knew it.

Silas knew it.

Asher tightened his grip on his gun.

Bring it, you bastard.

Silas spun into view with fluid speed. One minute the doorway was empty, the next Silas popped up like some pistol-packing jack-in-the-box. Asher dropped to one knee in a combat crouch as Silas blazed away with a Glock 17. Unsure of Asher's exact location, Silas capped off rounds in a random spray-and-pray pattern. A lamp exploded. Holes peppered the walls. Sheet-rock dust billowed into the air. A reproduction of *The Last Supper* fell to the floor, bullet holes drilled through the heads of Jesus, Judas, and other assorted apostles.

Asher possessed a distinct advantage—he knew right where Silas was. He framed his former friend in the HK's gunsights and hit the trigger.

Silas, realizing he had exposed himself for a split second too long, tried to duck back into the hallway. The .45 slug tore into the door jamb, shredded the wood, and hurled a storm of needle-edged splinters into his face. Silas let out a horrible cry as one of those slivers drove straight into his left eye. Asher caught a quick glimpse of spurting blood and then Silas moved out of the line of fire. But Asher could still hear the raw, wet howls of a man in excruciating pain.

And then...nothing.

Drops of Silas' blood dripped down the splintered doorframe as Asher waited for his enemy's next move. Smoke curled from the barrel of his .45 in a blue-gray twist. A long minute of silence ticked by with no further sounds from Silas.

"Is he gone?" Larissa asked.

"Not sure." Gun up and at the ready, Asher crossed the living room to the wrecked doorway. Carefully, not wanting to get his head blown off if Silas was still out there, he looked out into the hall. A trail of blood droplets led to the stairs. Looked like Silas had fled to lick his wounds.

Asher holstered his HK45 and returned to Larissa as sirens wailed in the distance. "We have to get out of here."

She slipped her hand into his. "All right, let's go."

Asher led her toward the exit as the sirens grew louder. He picked up the pace, pulling her along, then paused as she stumbled over Sirius.

"Hold on," she said, her voice choked with emotion, soft and fragile as butterfly wings. She knelt beside the dead dog, stroking his fur with a familiarity that came from years of companionship. "I can't just leave him like this."

"No choice," said Asher. "I'm sorry."

"I have to say goodbye."

The sirens shrilled in his ear. "You'll have to make it quick."

She leaned over and kissed the top of the dog's head as she hugged his neck for the last time. "Goodbye, Sirius. I'll never forget you. *Never*."

The sirens reached a critical crescendo. They were

out of time. Asher touched her shoulder. "Larissa, I'm sorry, but..."

She nodded, brushed the tears from her face, and stood up. As he led her away from the shattered remnants of her life, Asher knew that neither of their lives would ever be the same again.

CHAPTER 11

ASHER STEERED the Jeep Wrangler Sahara down I-87 as quickly as he dared without risking getting pulled over. A couple horns blared and a few middle fingers shot up but he ignored them. Right now, all that mattered was putting some distance between himself and Larissa and the carnage back at her apartment.

He pulled his eyes off the highway long enough to glance at Larissa, silent as stone in the shotgun seat. She gripped the dashboard so tightly that her knuckles turned white. Her face was pale and ghostly. Maybe it was his driving, but Asher suspected she was in post-traumatic shock. The loss of Sirius, her near-rape, the explosion of violence...it had all crashed down on her, leaving her shaken, dull, and lifeless.

Asher felt a streak of anger run through him. He wasn't a religious man, but he did believe God existed, and right now Asher wanted to ask Him just how much suffering He was going to shovel down on Larissa's head. He wanted to look God dead in the eye and ask, *How much is enough?*

In his anger, he stomped the gas a little harder. The sudden acceleration pinned Larissa back in her seat. Her nails dug deeper into the dash but still she said nothing, maintaining her haunted silence.

About twenty miles outside of Albany, the traffic thinned, and Asher set the cruise control at a respectable, non-attention-grabbing speed. His mind turned to thoughts of Macklin and Black Talon. Their dawn strike at his apartment a few days ago had failed but believing that was the end of the matter would be as foolish as trying to find a virgin in a brothel. Macklin was a ruthless machine who lived for the thrill of the hunt and the narcotic rush of the kill. He would just keep on coming, the Energizer Bunny of assassins.

Asher knew there would be no peace until either he or Macklin was dead. Their destinies were on a terminal collision course. He felt a bone-deep weariness. So much killing behind him, but so much more to be done.

No rest for the wicked, he thought.

"Where are we going?"

The sound of Larissa's voice pulled Asher from his grim thoughts. He glanced at her. She didn't look much better but at least she was talking. That was a good sign.

"We'll hole up at a hotel," Asher said. "Not sure which one yet." He knew enough to avoid the big chain hotels that lined the major highways, but how far from home should they run? His instincts said not far at all. They were being hunted by multiple parties—not just Silas and the Giadellos, but Macklin and Black Talon as well—and Asher preferred to face a fight on familiar turf. Stick to home ground rather than run and they might just gain an edge in a game in which every edge counted. Their hunters might not anticipate such a move.

Larissa lapsed back into silence, blinded eyes staring lifelessly out the window. Asher hated seeing her this way. She was a strong, vibrant woman, always ready with a laugh, and seeing her spirit broken like this infuriated him.

Impulsively, he reached out and touched her shoulder. Just a quick, comforting touch, and then he pulled his hand back.

Larissa turned toward him, eyes bright with tears. "Thank you," she said softly.

Asher nodded. No more words were needed.

———

Twenty minutes later, Asher pulled the Jeep into the garage. As he hit the remote to close the door, he said to Larissa, "I've got to grab some gear. We won't be here long. This is one of the first places they'll look for us, so we'll be in and out in five."

Larissa nodded. "Whatever you say. I'm just along for the ride. This is your area of expertise, not mine."

He helped her out of the Jeep, up the stairs into the kitchen, and guided her to a chair at the table. "Here," he said, "have a seat."

"I think I would rather just walk around, check out the place." Her head swiveled from side to side as if she could actually see. Only her unfocused eyes gave away her blindness.

Asher tried to keep his voice as gentle as he could. "Listen, we don't have a lot of time and right now saving our asses is a bit more important than giving you the ten-dollar tour."

"You can take that condescending tone and shove it up that ass you're trying to save." She smiled to take the caustic edge off her words. "I don't need a tour. Just go about your business and let me wander around."

Asher admired her fiery independence. He couldn't remember the last time someone had told him to shove something up his ass. Life might have kicked Larissa in the teeth, but she was still a fighter.

He went into his bedroom, pulled a large duffel bag out of the closet, and began loading up. As he did, he heard Larissa make her way into the adjoining bathroom. He glanced at her as she passed the bedroom doorway. Her hands were stretched out in front of her, guiding her through the unfamiliarity of her surroundings.

Asher felt a fresh surge of anger at Macklin. Executing rogue assassins, men with blood on their hands, was one thing. But putting bullets into innocents was something else, something evil, a violation of all that Asher held sacred.

He tossed some spare magazines for the HK45 into the duffel bag. Some people packed extra socks; he packed extra ammo.

Larissa called to him from the bathroom, her voice soft and hesitant. "Is this where..." She let the question hang, perhaps realizing she had no right to ask it.

The question stung, but he knew she had not meant to hurt him. "Yeah," he said, "that's where it happened."

"I'm sorry, I didn't mean..."

"It's okay. Really."

She appeared in the doorway as he added boxes of

shotgun shells to the duffel bag. "Todd and I wanted to come to the funeral," she said, "but we weren't sure if you wanted to see us or not, so I just sent a card. I'm sure you don't remember, but..." Her voice trailed off and it was clear she didn't know what else to say.

"I remember," Asher lied. He remembered a lot of things about that day. He remembered the grief that tore his heart in two. He remembered hating God for taking Karen away and at the same time he remembered thanking God for the cold rain when they buried her because it hid his tears. He remembered how few people had turned out to pay their final respects to his wife. He remembered thinking that he had done this to her, forced her into a life of isolation, without family, without children, without friends, and now there was nobody to stand beside her grave and say goodbye. He did not, however, remember who sent him sympathy cards. But there was no reason to hurt Larissa's feelings by telling her that. He took some fragmentation grenades from the top shelf of the closet and added them to the growing pile of firepower.

"Why do you have roses in your fridge?"

The question caught Asher off guard. "They're for my work," he said as he tossed a few bricks of C-4 into the bag. "I use white roses as a calling card."

"Why white roses?"

Asher zipped up the bag. "Because they were Karen's favorite."

"Do you think she would approve?"

"Don't know and she's not here to ask." Asher slung the bag over his shoulder. "Come on, let's get out of here."

Once they were back on the road, Larissa said,

"What about this Jeep? Won't they be looking for a vehicle matching this description?"

"That's why we're ditching it," Asher said. "I'll drop you off at a motel and then go find another set of wheels."

They drove into the town of Fort Edward, named after the colonial garrison that had once stood nearby. A mile up the road they pulled into the White Pine Motel, a seedy establishment located off the town's main drag. Asher had no clue why the place was named the White Pine Motel, for it wasn't white and there were no pine trees in sight. The place served as a flophouse for the local whores to turn their tricks, the kind of place where cash was king, you paid by the hour, and you didn't want to examine the bedsheets too closely.

Asher knew that no matter where they holed up, Silas would eventually find them. The best they could hope to gain was a little time. At least a few hours, a couple of days if they got lucky. But sooner rather than later, they would have to run.

The clerk—and probably part-time pimp—behind the desk was a short, fat man in his late forties. A small fan whirred away on the corner of the desk, but it didn't seem to be doing much good; the man's stray wisps of black, sweaty hair clung to his otherwise bald head like a wet cobweb and his grime-white T-Shirt clung to his fat rolls like sausage skin. He glanced up from his vintage, dog-eared copy of *Hustler* as Asher and Larissa walked in. He looked at Asher with boredom, but stripped Larissa with his eyes. Asher seriously considered breaking his face.

"Need a room," Asher said, glancing around at

what passed for a lobby. Cigarette butts and condom wrappers littered the floor.

"I'll just bet ya do," the clerk leered. His right hand stayed out of sight behind the desk, no doubt doing something obscene. With his left hand, he slid a thin, hard-cover book across the desk. "Care to sign the register?"

"No."

"Why am I not surprised?" the clerk drawled sarcastically. "Nobody ever wants to sign my register and when they do, it's always Jones or Smith." He pulled his hand away from his crotch long enough to reach behind him and pluck a key off the rack. He turned back to Asher and jerked his double chins toward Larissa. "So what's her story, huh? Her eyes look all screwed up. She blind or something?"

"Obviously *you're* not." Asher found the clerk's crassness as repulsive as his body odor. "Give me the key."

"Jeez." The clerk gave him an *excuse-the-hell-outa-me* look. "What's up your butt, pal? I was just making conversation."

"If I want conversation, I'll join a chat room," Asher said. "So do yourself a favor and mind your own business."

The clerk held out his hand, room-key dangling from his fingers. But when Asher went to take it, the fat man jerked it back just out of his reach and gave Asher a taunting grin. "This place *is* my business, pal, and I wanna know what kind of girl you're entertaining." He jingled the key mockingly. "After all, I can't allow some skank ho to ply her trade here, now can I? Not in a fine, upscale establishment such as this." He jingled the key again.

Asher's asshole tolerance levels had bottomed out. "This place is full of skank whores," he rasped, "so cut the crap and give me the key before I kick your balls through the bottom of your spine."

"Oh, my." The clerk held out his hand and shook it with an exaggerated motion, making the keys jingle yet again. "I'm so scared I'm shaking. I think I'm gonna piss my pants, you scared me so much."

Asher struck like a cobra. His fingers closed around the clerk's wrist so tight he could feel the man's pulse.

"Hey!" The clerk's piggish eyes bulged from their sockets. "Let go of me, you motherf—"

Asher wrenched the man's wrist, grinding bones. The clerk's obscenity became a hiss of pain. His fingers spasmed open. The key clattered to the desk top. Asher reached for it with his free hand.

But as his fingers closed around it, Larissa covered his hand with her own. "Enough," she said. "Let him go."

Asher's anger immediately ebbed. He felt the warmth of her hand and though it was just an innocent touch, he felt himself wanting to respond to it. But he knew he could never allow himself to open up to another woman again.

He pulled his hand away from hers, released the clerk with a shove, and turned away, black duster swirling around him like the shadows around his heart.

———

They holed up in the room for the day, surviving on granola bars and bottled water from the vending machine. When evening arrived, Asher ventured out and fetched supper from a nearby greasy spoon. He returned with a feast of blackened hockey-puck hamburgers, half-cooked French fries, and tepid soda. They sat at the table by the window but kept the blinds closed. The glow from the motel's sputtering neon sign cast a pink hue on the glass.

Larissa bit into a fry. It crunched like a carrot stick. She made a face, then smiled. "You know what this reminds me of?"

"What?" Asher tentatively tried a burger. Burnt on the outside, bleeding in the middle. A steaming pile of dog crap would probably taste better.

"Our first date. Remember?"

Asher grinned. "Yeah, I remember. I take you out to one of the finest steakhouses in the city and what do you order? A burger and fries."

"Not fries—potato slices sautéed in a special wine sauce. They were supposed to be a house specialty. The waiter recommended them. Too bad he forgot to mention they would be served raw!"

"That's okay. I tipped him with a fake fifty from my last assignment."

Larissa laughed and Asher was glad to hear the sound. Pain still haunted her eyes, but the numbing shock that had gripped her since the attack at her apartment seemed to have eased up.

Then her laughter trailed off and her face got somber. In a very quiet voice, she said, "You know, that was also the first night you ever kissed me."

Asher said nothing and a heavy, awkward chasm of

silence opened up between them. He pushed aside his food, no longer hungry. He turned his head and looked out the window. The darkness beckoned to him.

He abruptly pushed back his chair. "I have to go." The walls were closing in on him. There was simply too much history in the room.

Larissa said, "Hey, I'm sorry, I didn't mean to—"

He cut her off. "It's fine. I just need some air. And I still have to get us some new wheels. I'll leave the shotgun, so you should be fine. Don't open the door for anyone but me."

Larissa looked like she wanted to say something, but instead just bit her lower lip and nodded.

Once outside, Asher let the cool evening wash over him and tried to let go of his resentment toward Larissa. What did she want from him? Their time together had been brief and those days were long gone. She needed to stop trying to build a bridge between their past and present. It wouldn't work. It *couldn't* work.

Asher got into the Jeep and headed for the country, leaving the lights of town behind. His headlamps stabbed the darkness and every now and then he heard the wet splat of insects dying against his windshield. Turmoil tormented his mind and jumbled his mental processes.

He punched the steering wheel in frustration. Having Larissa come back into his life had really messed him up. Especially since her return was so unexpected, so improbable, that it defied all odds and bordered on the miraculous. And that begged thoughts of God, fate, destiny; in other words, things he didn't want to think about.

He drove through his old haunts, past the fields and

farms where he and Silas had played together as boys during simpler, more innocent times. They had been blissfully unaware of how much pain awaited them down the road, that their friendship would end in dust and ashes.

Asher sped past Rowe Hill and glanced up the hill at the Perelli estate, crouched above the hamlet like some medieval castle. Lights shone in the windows and Asher had little doubt that Rene Perelli sat behind one of those windows, plotting her next move against Frank Giadello.

A mile up the road he came to Morningside Cemetery. He parked the Jeep just outside the wrought-iron gates and walked up the path. A sickle-shaped moon carved through thin, wispy clouds and Asher could feel its cold light and see its stark reflection on the endless array of marble gravestones and stone angels. Dead leaves scuttled across his path, the sound startlingly loud in the stillness of this barren land of ghosts and memories.

When he reached the grave he had come to visit, he reached down and traced the inscription, shadows pooling in the etched letters.

KAREN J. ASHER
1979-2015
LIFE
LOVE
DEATH
WE HAVE KNOWN THEM ALL

He had carved the words into the stone with his own hands. This was his sanctuary, his place of solace, where he came to find slivers of peace. Touching the gravestone made him feel closer to Karen.

A twig snapped behind him. He started to turn but before he could, he felt a gun pressed against the back of his head. He froze, fingers inches from his own firearm.

"Take your gun out." A male voice, so harsh and raspy the words were barely intelligible; the guy sounded like he gargled with broken glass. "Do it slowly. Two fingers and neither of them should go near the trigger."

Asher complied. Not like he had a choice.

"Remove the mag and give it to me."

Asher popped the magazine and handed it back over his shoulder. It was snatched out of his hand and tossed into the darkness. He heard it bounce off a gravestone to his left.

"Now throw your gun in the opposite direction."

"You forgot to say please," Asher said, but he tossed the .45 off to his right.

"A guy on the wrong end of a magnum shouldn't run his mouth."

Asher felt the gun lift away from his head and then savage pain blasted through his skull. As he fell to the ground, banging his forehead against Karen's tombstone and splitting open the skin, he realized he had just been pistol-whipped. Groaning, he crawled into a sitting position, his back against Karen's marker. Blood ran into his eye. He wiped it away and looked up at his attacker.

A tall man dressed in a black bomber jacket, holding a stainless-steel .357 Magnum revolver. His face, tinted silver by the moonlight, consisted of sharp angles and rugged lines. But it was not the face that drew Asher's attention, but what was beneath it. A thick line of scar tissue curled across the man's throat like a vicious smile, the sort of wound not even the devil himself should have been able to walk away from. "I'll be damned," Asher said. "Macklin."

"So you know who I am."

Asher's skull throbbed with pain. "I thought you couldn't speak."

"A myth. When the Colombians cut my throat, they damaged my vocal cords, which is why I sound like I do. But I can still speak."

Asher studied the vicious scar. "How did you even survive that?"

Macklin's chuckle sounded like razor blades grinding together. "Believe what you will, because you would never believe the truth."

"Try me."

"Not today."

"Fine." Asher looked the assassin dead in the eye. "Make it quick, you son of a bitch."

"I didn't come here tonight to kill you," Macklin said. "I came to pay my respects to your wife."

Something in the way he said it made Asher's skin crawl.

"But rest assured," Macklin continued, "that one day I *will* kill you and I hope you die more quietly than your wife did."

Asher's eyes narrowed. "What did you just say?"

"Your wife," Macklin repeated. "She died screaming your name."

"How the fuck do you know how my wife died?" But even as he asked the question, Asher knew the answer, sensed the terrible truth, the dark revelation that everything he believed about Karen's death was a lie. The pieces came together swiftly in his mind. Karen had not killed herself; she had been murdered by Macklin who masked her death as a suicide.

He imagined Karen screaming as Macklin opened her wrists and felt something inside his soul curdle and die. A single burning question rose in his mind. He looked into Macklin's cold, shark-like eyes and asked, "Why?"

"Because she was there," Macklin said. "I actually came for you that day, but you weren't home, so I played with your wife instead. I did it to fuck with you, Gabriel, simple as that."

In a voice barren as bleached bone, Asher said, "You're going to die, Macklin. I'm going to take your life from you."

Macklin's breath plumed in the brisk air. "You can't kill what is immortal, Asher. I am a force of nature, an act of God, and you are mine. I can take you at will. The only reason you continue to breathe is because I enjoy the game, the hunt. You are the best the Company has ever seen, by far the best prey I have ever had the pleasure of pursuing. You are my trophy, Asher, and in the end, I will take you down. But not until I have broken you, taken from you everything and everyone you hold dear."

Asher knew he had just glimpsed the inner mechanisms of Macklin's twisted mind. "You're one sick son of a bitch," he said.

"And you're a dead man who will spend the rest of your existence with an itch between your shoulder blades, always wondering when the bullet with your name on it will come calling."

Asher tried to stand up. He imagined he could hear Karen in the cold grave beneath him, crying out for vengeance. The thought nearly drove him insane.

The muzzle of Macklin's .357 Magnum thudded against Asher's forehead, driving him back down into a sitting position. "Don't be a fool," Macklin said. "I could kill you before you even got to your feet."

"I'm not afraid to die. Hell, there are some days I think about doing it myself."

"Next time you think about it, go ahead and get it done. It will save me a bullet."

Asher exploded into motion. A suicide play, sure, but he didn't care. He was too full of fury to sit still any longer. He had to do *something*, even if that something got him killed. He threw himself toward his tossed gun. No magazine, but there was still a bullet in the chamber. And one bullet was all he needed.

He heard the heavy tread of Macklin's boots behind him. Why didn't the bastard just shoot him? Asher waited for the roar of the revolver. At this range, the .357 would blow his spine right in two. Not a nice way to die.

Asher's hand closed around his HK. Knowing he had no chance but determined to try anyway, he rolled onto his back and raised the gun. The black bore of Macklin's Magnum filled his vision. The hammer was cocked. Less than a pound of pressure and the revolver would fire.

Asher aimed the HK45 at the ugly scar on Macklin's throat, but there was no way to kill Macklin without dying himself. Even if he put one right through Macklin's head, the nerves would go spastic, compress the .357's trigger, and turn Asher's face into dog food.

He would have his vengeance, but was it worth the price?

"Before you decide whether or not to pull that trigger," Macklin said, "there's something you should know. Right now, one of my men is keeping your new lady friend company."

Asher's jaw clenched.

"So," Macklin continued, "you can shoot me, but the girl will die. Because if I don't call my man and tell him I am safe, then his orders are to put two bullets in her head. Normally I would say only one, but since she proved once before that one bullet to her head isn't enough to kill her, I told my man to use two this time. I hate making the same mistake twice."

Asher lowered his gun. There was no other choice. He could not sacrifice Larissa's life on the altar of his own vengeance.

Macklin smirked. "Ain't love grand?"

"Just so we're clear, Macklin, I'm going to nail your fucking ass to the wall."

"Maybe, but not tonight. Looks like tonight we both live to die another day." Macklin lowered the Magnum. "Wait here for fifteen minutes. Once I'm convinced you're not following me, I'll call my man and he'll leave your girlfriend."

"Her name is Larissa."

Macklin walked backwards until the darkness swallowed him. His voice floated out of the shadows. "She's just another blind bitch to me, Asher."

Asher crawled around in the dark for the next five minutes, searching for his magazine. When he finally found it, there was a slight ding in the metal where the magazine had struck the stone. But it was just cosmetic damage, nothing that would prevent it from working.

Asher slammed the magazine up the well of the .45. He wished he could empty every last round into Macklin's body. He had learned secrets tonight, secrets that demanded a reckoning.

He walked over and put his hand on his wife's marker. *One day,* he vowed, *I'll settle all debts with that son of a bitch.*

He waited in the cemetery another ten minutes and then ran to the Jeep. It was twenty minutes back to the motel. As his headlights carved through the night, Asher knew they were going to be the longest twenty minutes of his life.

CHAPTER 12

WHEN ASHER OPENED the door to the motel room, he found the gaping bore of a shotgun shoved in his face. So close that if he licked his lips, he would end up French-kissing the muzzle. He instantly froze and said, "Larissa, it's me."

With a look of relief, she lowered the SPAS-12. "Better safe than sorry." Her apologetic smile softened her features and amplified her beauty.

"When did he leave?"

Larissa laid the shotgun on the bed. "Who?"

"The guy who was here."

"What are you talking about?"

He told her what had happened.

"There was nobody here," she said.

Asher realized he had fallen for a bluff. He could practically hear Macklin laughing his ass off right now. He took off his duster, sat down on the edge of the bed, and clasped his head in his hands. It wasn't possible to hate someone more than he hated Macklin right now. This hatred eclipsed even the hate he felt toward Silas.

Asher abruptly realized some of his hatred toward his former best friend was misplaced. He had spent five long years believing Silas had not only bedded Karen but had also caused her to take her own life. But that sin did not belong to Silas, it belonged to Macklin.

He felt something inside tugging at him to forgive Silas, to lay the past to rest. But he had hated the man for so long that he didn't know how to *not* hate him. Besides, Macklin might have murdered Karen, but Silas had still slept with her, and that was not something Asher could just sweep under the rug.

Lost in his thoughts, Asher didn't realize Larissa was standing in front of him until she soothingly touched his face. He winced when her fingers found the gash above his eye where he had fallen against Karen's gravestone. "You're hurt," she said.

"Just a scalp wound. No big deal."

"Well, come into the bathroom and let me clean you up."

Asher followed her into the bathroom and sat on the lowered toilet lid while she ran a washcloth under some hot water. She wrung it out and turned to him. "Hold still." She leaned forward and found the cut with remarkable accuracy for a blind woman. She gently scrubbed away the crusted blood.

Her closeness made Asher uncomfortable. She was close enough for him to feel the heat of her body, smell the scent of her skin, and both were leading him down a road of thoughts best left untraveled. The bathroom suddenly seemed stifling hot.

He abruptly stood up and pushed her aside, rougher than intended. Larissa stumbled and grabbed the towel rack to keep from falling. Asher instantly felt lower than snail shit. "Larissa, I'm sorry."

She looked shocked and angry but more than anything else she looked hurt. "What the hell is wrong with you?" she snapped.

"Nothing," he said. "I just...you and I..." He shook his head. "We just need to get out of here."

"I haven't finished cleaning your cut."

"It'll have to be good enough." Asher exited the bathroom. "We need to hit the road. Talon knows where we are."

"Sometimes I think Talon will always know where we are." Larissa followed him out of the bathroom. "So where are we going now?"

Asher shrugged on his duster, slung the duffel bag over his shoulder, and picked up the shotgun. "We'll figure it out."

"Did you get a new vehicle?"

"No, the Jeep will have to do for now." Asher felt fresh blood welling up in the gash over his eye and wiped it away. Once they found someplace to hole up he would have Larissa put a couple stitches in it. Another scar for his collection. He reached for the door knob, then froze.

Larissa sensed his tension. "What is it?"

Asher listened to the *whap-whap-whap* of approaching rotor blades. Their numbers had just run down to zero. "Chopper," he said.

"Talon?"

"Who else?" Asher felt the hot rush of pre-combat adrenalin surge through him in sharp contrast to the coldness of self-rage. Like a fool, he'd played right into

Macklin's hands, allowing himself to be herded back to Larissa so that Macklin could take them both out at the same time. The bastard could have easily killed him at the cemetery and then offed Larissa at his leisure, but that wasn't good enough for a brain-twisted psychopath like Macklin. He wanted Asher to hold another dead woman in his arms. That was Macklin's warped, sick little game and Asher had played along like a puppet blind to the hand jerking his strings. The thought royally pissed him off and drove him into explosive action.

He dragged Larissa down between the beds. The chopper hovered right outside, rotor blades concussing the air, the sound deafening. The window suddenly exploded, blown apart by machinegun-fire. A .50 caliber, judging from its sound. Bullets chewed into the beds, shredding the sheets and pillows.

Asher pressed his hand against Larissa's back, keeping her pinned to the floor. He could feel her trembling. "Keep your head down!" he said as he drew his HK45 and raised his own head just enough to see the chopper hovering outside the shattered window. The rotor-wash whipped up clouds of churning dust from the parking lot, forcing Asher to squint through the grit.

A spotlight mounted on a swivel under the chopper's nose powered up and probed the room with a lance of harsh white light. Asher immediately double-tapped two rounds straight up the beam. The light went out in a burst of glass and sparks. Right now, darkness was their ally and Asher wanted all he could get.

He dropped back down between the two bullet-riddled beds as the machine-gunner strafed the room again. Huge holes appeared in the walls. The flimsy furniture exploded like matchsticks. The .50 caliber would decimate the room in no time.

They had to get the hell out of here.

The instant the machinegun stopped hammering, Asher rose and fired six shots at the black shape behind the .50. He saw the target jerk to the side as a slug clipped his shoulder. The machinegun swung wildly on its mount as Asher dumped the rest of the magazine into the guy's head, punching him backward with his skull turned into a blood-spewing colander.

Asher quickly ejected the spent magazine, grabbed a fresh one from the duffel bag, and slammed it up the well. As he jacked a round into the chamber, he knew they only had a few seconds before another gunner replaced the dead man at the .50.

He grabbed Larissa by the arm and pulled her to her feet. "Let's go!"

When he opened the door, a dust-storm whipped into the room. Squinting against the stinging spray, he saw that the chopper hovered directly over the Jeep, the vehicle's outline just barely visible through the haze of dust from the rotor-wash. If they could make it to the Jeep, the chopper's own belly would shield them for a few seconds, give them a chance to escape. A slim chance, sure, but Asher would take it. There were no other options.

He glanced up through the dust and debris. Someone else now manned the machinegun because its muzzle swung toward him, seeking target acquisition.

They had to move. *Now*.

He grabbed Larissa's hand and ran for the Jeep.

The night exploded with noise as the machine-gunner opened fire. A stream of .50 caliber slugs nipped at their heels, gouging holes in the parking lot. Asher felt pieces of pulverized pavement pluck at his legs like shrapnel.

Then they were under the chopper, out of the line of fire. They scrambled into the Jeep as the chopper crabbed to the right, maneuvering to give the gunner a clear shot. The Jeep would provide little protection from the .50. The massive rounds would tear the vehicle apart like a tin can. They had to get the hell out of here and fast.

The tires smoked as he dropped the Jeep into reverse and whipped it around in a tight arc. He then shifted into Drive and punched the gas. He took a left out of the motel parking lot and sped up the hill past the local high school, heading towards Hudson Falls, the next town over. He needed to find some open road where he could maneuver.

He barreled into Hudson Falls at 85 mph, weaving in and out of traffic. As he whipped past the town park, the screech of his tires reverberated off the clustered storefronts lining the street. Pedestrians tossed annoyed glances at him. Annoyance turned to shock when they were nearly bowled off their feet by the chopper flashing just above the roofs in hot pursuit.

Asher couldn't actually see the chopper, but he could hear it, clinging to his wake like the shadow of some aerial dragon. His mind raced, sifting through options, discarding them all until there was only one choice left. With no way to lose the chopper, he had to find a way to bring it down.

At the edge of town, the road he currently traveled

turned into Route 4, a long stretch of country road that wove through a series of tiny hamlets. Little occupied this stretch save for farms and fields. Here he could make his play with minimal risk of innocents getting caught in the crossfire.

He hit the town limits in less than ninety seconds, whipped across a four-way intersection onto Route 4 and barely avoided being broadsided by a semi. The trucker blasted his air-horn in irritation, but it was drowned out by the roar of the chopper overhead.

The .50 rattled to life, punching holes in the roof of the Jeep. More bullets blew out the back window, spraying shards into the night.

Larissa flinched as the slugs slammed through metal and glass. She gripped the dashboard. Her face was white. Her knuckles were even whiter. "That was close, wasn't it?"

"Too close." Asher fought to control the Jeep as it raced around a curve. The rear end wanted to slide. The steering wheel shuddered in his hands. The Jeep fishtailed as it came out of the curve. The tires howled in protest as Asher brought it back under control. Cold sweat trickled down his face, stung his eyes.

He wrenched the wheel to the left as another salvo shot from the chopper's gun. The slugs missed, slicing into the road. The machine-gunner corrected his aim and tracked a line of fire across the Jeep's roof again. Bullets pounded into the rear compartment. The leather seats exploded as if Semtex had been buried in the cushions. Larissa screamed and Asher didn't blame her.

They barreled into the hamlet of Kingsbury at 80 mph, little more than a handful of houses clustered around a country deli and a little white church. On the other side, the road straightened, unfolding before the Jeep's headlights like a long black ribbon.

Asher glanced in the rearview mirror. The chopper still clung to their tail, a deadly black mass in the sky. But it had dropped lower, now skimming above the road just slightly higher than the Jeep's roof.

Which gave Asher an idea.

He held out his right hand to Larissa. "Grenade."

"What?"

"A grenade. Give me a grenade."

Larissa dug around in the duffel bag at her feet. After a few moments she pulled out a fragmentation grenade and slapped it into Asher's waiting palm. He transferred the grenade to his left hand and lowered the driver's side window. Cool night air rushed into the cab along with the roar of the chopper.

He glanced in the rearview mirror again. The chopper was still in position. Asher knew he would only get one shot at this. He could see the reflection of stars scattered across the Plexiglas canopy and could just make out the shadow-shape of the pilot inside, doing his best to get Asher killed.

Okay, asshole, let's see how you like this.

He braced his left knee against the bottom of the steering wheel to keep the Jeep straight long enough for him to pull the pin on the grenade. The arming spoon sprang out, triggering the timer. Five seconds to detonation. Asher held it for three, then thrust his arm out the window and tossed the grenade backwards and *up*. He doubted the pilot even saw it coming.

It exploded directly in front of the chopper.

Hot shrapnel shredded the canopy. Sliced through

the console. Scythed into the pilot's neck and head. In the hands of a dead man, the chopper lurched like a drunken bird, the rotor blades beating the air like impotent wings as smoke poured from the crippled cockpit.

Asher glanced at Larissa. He had seen mimes with better skin color. He reached out and touched her hand. "It's over," he said. "I got 'em."

"Really?"

"Really."

In the rearview mirror, Asher watched the chopper weaving erratically, spinning first left, then right, inexorably losing what little altitude it had, dipping closer and closer to the ground.

Come on, you bastards, Asher thought. *Eat asphalt.* He wanted to see the chopper smash into the ground and erupt into a fireball that would signal the end of Black Talon. He just hoped Macklin lived long enough to smell his own burning flesh.

The ground rushed up at the big metal bird. The landing skids slammed into the pavement. The chopper bounced back into the air and then dipped again, simultaneously rolling to the right like a dying whale. The rotor blades caught in the thick steel guardrail cables and shattered in a flurry of debris. The sudden impact drove the tail into the ground, snapping the rear rotors. The skids hit the road again and buckled, dropping the chopper onto its belly. Sparks flew where metal met blacktop until the chopper came to a grinding halt in the middle of Route 4. No fiery explosion, but the next vehicle that came along was in for quite a surprise.

Asher turned his attention back to the road. Beside him, Larissa was quiet, lost in her own thoughts, whatever they might be. He rolled up the window, cutting off the cold wind rushing through the bullet-strafed Jeep as the headlights peeled back the night. He wasn't sure where they were going, but that didn't matter. All that mattered was that Talon was a fading image in his rearview mirror.

For now, anyway.

CHAPTER 13

TEN MINUTES and a dozen miles later, a light ground fog began creeping across the road, forcing Asher to slow down. They had just passed through the quiet village of Fort Ann and now entered the hamlet of Comstock. Off to the right, the harsh white lights of the Great Meadow Correctional Facility gleamed menacingly on rows of razor wire. Asher knew that he might end up behind those walls someday. He had executed more men than he cared to count and if he ever found himself before a judge, it would not matter that all his victims had deserved to die. They would call him a conscienceless killer and drag him away in chains to spend the rest of his life in a cage.

He would rather eat a bullet.

Larissa spoke, pulling him back from his bleak thoughts. "I know where we can go."

Asher glanced at her. Her face had regained some color; she no longer looked like a ghost. "Where?" he asked, as they passed a sign that indicated the town of Whitehall was only ten miles up ahead.

"Grampy Cobby's," she said. "I told you, he lives in an old hunting cabin way back in the woods. It's the perfect place to hole up, at least until we can come up with long-term plans."

Asher remembered her saying that Cobb now lived off the grid in the backwoods of Dresden, which was only about fifteen miles up the road between Whitehall and Ticonderoga. He didn't like involving an innocent in their dangerous situation, but if Cobb was as isolated as Larissa indicated, it was unlikely Talon would find them any time soon. "All right," he said, "let's do it."

"Once you go through Whitehall, look for Pike Brook Road on your left," she directed.

Whitehall looked deserted when they drove through it. The only spots that appeared to be open were a convenience store, laundromat, and a rundown motel uncreatively called Joe's Motel. The motel boasted a big, illuminated sign out front, but only half the lights worked, so the sign read Jo Mo. Knowing they needed to ditch the bullet-riddled Jeep, Asher swung into the parking lot. There were no cars out front, but back behind the office they found a well-kept '95 Dodge Ram pickup that probably belonged to the owner of the motel. Asher wasn't surprised to find the doors unlocked and the keys tucked above the visor; it was that kind of town.

Vehicle swap completed, he drove through the town's sole traffic light, then glanced over at Larissa. Her head was turned toward the window, as if she was gazing out at the dark scenery rolling by. Part of him wanted to ask her what she was thinking about, but he didn't want to risk stirring up an emotional hornet's nest.

Instead, he turned his thoughts to Silas, wondering if he was dead or alive. Asher had seen the sliver of wood impale Silas' eye, but it obviously hadn't killed him instantly. Had he succumbed to the wound later? Asher knew he would have to find out eventually. If Silas were dead, he could finally let go of his hate.

The road became a bridge over South Bay, the southern tip of Lake Champlain, and as Asher looked out across the water, he saw moonlight dancing over the glassy surface, mating with the fog to give the bay a spectral glow. On the other side of the bridge was Pike Brook Road. Asher took the left-hand turn and felt the pavement become rough and uneven, tires juddering over potholes. The truck's headlights flashed over fog-laced woods.

"I take it we're on Pike Brook Road," said Larissa.

Asher felt the shocks being punished by the rough road. "What was your first clue?"

"Hardly anyone lives back here," Larissa said, "so the county never bothers to fix the road. A half mile ahead you'll see an abandoned house on the left. You can't miss it. Place looks like a junkyard. When you see it, let me know."

"You sure your grandfather isn't going to mind us dropping in on him like this in the middle of the night?"

"Of course not. He'll be happy to have some company. You know, he always liked you. He'll be glad to have you back for a visit."

As long as the visit doesn't get him killed.

He spotted the abandoned house. With the skeletons of ancient automobiles rusting amidst the wild grass, thorn bushes, and heaping mounds of garbage, the place did indeed look like a junkyard. "We just passed that house," he said. "What am I looking for now?"

"There should be a clearing just up ahead on the right. Across from that is the path we want."

Asher noticed she said "path" and not "road". A few moments later he realized why. What had once been a logging road was now little more than a deeply rutted, rock-strewn path barely wide enough for a single vehicle. Asher engaged the four-wheel drive and drove slowly. Brush choked both sides of the trail, branches scraping against the truck like bony fingers.

The Dodge jerked and jolted over the nasty terrain as Larissa clung to the armrest like a drowning sailor clutching a life preserver. "Rougher than I remember," she said.

"How far to the cabin?" Asher asked.

"About a mile."

As the Dodge bucked its way up the trail, Asher thought about Matthew Cobb. He hadn't seen the old man since he and Larissa had split up. He wondered if Cobb blamed him for breaking his granddaughter's heart. Asher steeled himself for the possibility of awkward questions and angry accusations.

A few minutes later, Asher saw a "No Trespassing" sign nailed to a tree. He drove past it, splashed through a small stream that bisected the path, and then Cobb's cabin appeared off to the right, set back amid some pine trees. Asher didn't see any place to park so he just stopped in the middle of the path and killed the engine.

"Are we there?" Larissa asked.

"Yeah."

Just then the cabin door opened, spilling a wedge of light out onto the porch. A silhouette loomed in the doorway, a featureless black shape that Asher recognized as Cobb. His hand dropped to the butt of his .45 when he saw Cobb carried a shotgun, an automatic response, as involuntary as breathing. It would be pretty ironic to escape Talon's clutches only to be killed by friendly fire from a gun-happy grandpa.

"Don't know who you peckerwoods are," Cobb called out in a gruff voice, "or what you're doing with Joe's truck, but I suggest you haul butt back the way you came or I'll fill your asses with so much buckshot you'll be shitting lead for a week straight."

Larissa opened her door, activating the dome light. "Grampy, it's me. Put the gun down before you hurt yourself."

"Lissy? That you? By God, girl!" Cobb scampered down the porch steps with an agility that belied his advanced years. He strode toward the truck on a walkway made of pallets and planks. "Who's that with you? New beau?"

"More like an old one."

Asher opened his door and climbed out. "Hello, Matt."

"Gabriel Asher. Well, I'll be damned." Cobb's voice held no hostility and Asher realized he had been worried for nothing. "By God, boy, what brings you way back to these parts? A pansy like you could get himself killed sneaking 'round in this back-country."

"Long story," said Asher.

"And you'll tell me every last bit of it, but I reckon it'll hold until we get you two love-birds inside."

"We're not—"

Cobb waved a hand. "Save it, sonny. Get my granddaughter inside first and then you can tell me what is and what ain't."

As Asher circled around to the passenger side of the truck, he studied the cabin. A bit ramshackle, but not bad. About forty feet long, fifteen feet wide, constructed of rough-cut lumber. A chimney sprouted from the back corner of the roof, probably connected to a wood stove, judging from the firewood stacked next to the porch.

Thick mud sucked at Asher's boots as he opened Larissa's door and took her hand to help her out. Cobb stayed on the walkway, not saying anything, but Asher knew his eyes watched every move, missing nothing. That's just the kind of man Cobb was. Asher had no doubt that he was trying to decipher exactly where things stood with him and Larissa, and if he couldn't figure it out on his own, he would just come right out and ask.

Larissa stepped out of the truck and promptly sank up to her ankles in thick, sucking mud. She gasped as the cold muck oozed into her shoes. "I'm sinking!" She grabbed Asher's arm and clung to him.

Asher was acutely aware of her closeness. He swallowed hard and said, "So?"

"So," Larissa said with an impish grin, "you'll have to carry me to the cabin."

Asher knew he shouldn't, knew it would bring back memories best left buried. Those memories were already banging on the door of his mind, threatening to break through and tear open old scars. But he also knew he was going to do it anyway. Putting thought to action, he reached down and cradled her in his arms.

Instant flashback...

Their sixth date. Their first time making love. Just him and Larissa in a quiet motel far off the beaten path. Asher took her in his arms, desire making his heart ache. Larissa pulled his head down to hers. Their lips fused with wild emotion as they surrendered to each other, kissing their breath away, yielding to the magical spell of passion sweeping over them.

A single candle burned on the nightstand. Soft shadows flickered across the bed. Asher laid her down and they slowly undressed each other. She smiled up at him, and that smile said it all.

And then they were one, flesh on flesh, burning with a passion so intense he thought it would reduce him to smoldering ashes. She cried out in ecstasy, her body shuddering as she gasped into his ear that she would love him forever.

Cobb's voice broke through his memories, jerking him unceremoniously back to the present. "Well, are you just gonna stand there or are you gonna bring her inside?"

"Gabriel." Larissa kept her voice soft so Cobb couldn't hear. "Are you all right?"

"I'm fine. Just...thinking."

She raised a hand to touch his face, but he pulled away. "Don't," he said.

"Why not?"

Her question echoed in his mind.

Why not?

He would never tell her the truth. Because the truth was that he wanted her touch, her kiss, wanted to wipe away the dust and scars from his heart and dare to love again. But he could not allow that to happen. No matter how dangerously close Cupid's arrows came to stirring up feelings for Larissa, his heart belonged to Karen. Heaven or Hell, he had promised to love her forever and it was a promise he refused to break.

He carried Larissa through the mud and set her down on the walkway. Cobb scooped her into his arms and squeezed her so tight Asher thought he was going to crush her. But the beaming smile on her face made it clear she wasn't being hurt. Cobb picked her up and swung her around. "God, it's good to see you, Lissy."

"Grampy, put me down," Larissa said, laughing.

"I notice you didn't tell Asher to put you down when he was holding you," Cobb retorted with a mischievous twinkle in his eyes. But he obeyed his granddaughter's wishes and set her down on the walkway.

"That's because you're an old man, Grampy." Larissa grinned. "Asher's arms can handle my weight, but you have to be careful not to break something." She mimicked the sound of snapping bone, then stood on her toes and kissed Cobb's grizzled cheek.

Cobb snorted. "Who you calling old, missy? Asher, drag your scrawny little butt into that cabin right this instant, 'cause you and me are gonna have ourselves an honest-to-God arm-wrestling contest so I can prove to this sassy-mouthed granddaughter of mine that I can whup your ass any day of the week and twice on Sunday."

Asher had retrieved the duffel bag from the truck while listening to Larissa and Cobb's good-natured banter. He slung it over his shoulder and joined them on the walkway. "Think I'll pass on that, Matt. You scare me too much."

In the trees nearby, an owl hooted. Deeper in the

woods, some sort of prey screamed as it fell to a predator in the continual cycle of life and death. Out here, existence was reduced to its simplest form, and Asher found that soothing. A slight breeze stirred the pine needles above them. Asher knew better than to let his guard down, but maybe they had found a place they could actually rest for a few days.

Cobb put his arm around Larissa's shoulders and guided her toward the cabin. "Hear that, Lissy? Asher says I scare the piss outta him. Smart man."

Grinning, Asher followed them into the cabin. Cobb really had gone hermit, stripping away the trappings of civilization. The floor consisted of bare boards covered with cheap throw rugs. The walls were stuffed with pink insulation held up by a few strategically placed sheets of wood paneling. An ancient wood stove squatted in the corner, a rickety table and a couple of straight-backed chairs occupied the center of the room, and a gas stove and slop sink took up most of the west wall. Gas lamps hung here and there, copper tubing snaking along the exposed rafters. A half-wall with a doorway cut into it separated the kitchen/living area from Cobb's bedroom—or what passed for a bedroom in this ramshackle lodge.

"The Taj Mahal it ain't," said Cobb, "but I call it home. Got a couple of propane tanks out back for the lights and stove. Ain't no plumbing—sink just drains out under the cabin—so when you feel the need to bleed your bladder, you'll have to take a walk; outhouse is on the other side of the road." He deposited Larissa in a battered armchair next to the wood stove and then turned to Asher. "Of course, you and I being men and all, we can just step out on the porch and let it hang over the side. Nature is our urinal, ya know? But don't let me catch you asking Larissa to give you a hand, if you know what I mean."

"Grampy!" Larissa's cheeks flushed red.

Asher just shook his head and smiled. Cobb was a real piece of work. "I think I can handle things myself, Matt."

"You want to handle your thing yourself, that's your business. Just make sure you clean up after yourself." Cobb headed for the stove, his step spry and lively; he looked like a wizened old leprechaun. "Now, while I whip us up some java, go ahead and tell me just what brings you two all the way out here."

Asher gave him the bare-bones version. By the time Cobb fetched some mugs from the cupboard over the sink and filled them with fresh-brewed coffee, Asher had brought him up to speed.

Cobb set a steaming cup in front of Asher. "Hope you like it black, 'cause I'm all out of cream and sugar. Need to take a trip into town soon." He put a cup in Larissa's hands and then sat down at the table across from Asher. "One thing you should know. That Frank Giadello scumbag you mentioned? He's dead."

"How do you know?"

Cobb pointed at a small battery-operated radio sitting on a shelf. "Heard it on the news. They're speculating it was some kind of gangland rivalry, one crime family taking out another. They nailed Giadello right in front of his house, just outside the gates. Took out two bodyguards and then proceeded to put some serious killing into him. News report said he was hit by over twenty bullets, so somebody really wanted him dead."

"Rene Perelli," Larissa said.

Asher nodded. "Sounds like she finally got some payback."

"And then some," Cobb said. "So you can scratch him off your list of worries."

"You catch the names of the two bodyguards?"

"Yeah, uh, just give me a minute." Cobb's brow wrinkled for a few moments, then he snapped his fingers. "Torlini," he said. "Andrew, maybe? Can't think of the other guy's name, but I'm pretty sure it was French or something like that."

"Jean-Luc?"

"Yeah, that's it."

Asher leaned back in his chair. "So Silas is still alive."

"You don't know that," Cobb countered. "He could be worm food by now. And even if he is alive, you took out his eye, for God's sake."

"All the more reason for him to come looking for me." Asher watched a moth, drawn by the light, thump against the window, beating its powdery wings to tatters against the glass.

"He really hate you that much?" Cobb asked, taking a sip of coffee.

"When it comes to me and Silas, hate might not be a strong enough word."

Cobb set his cup back down on the table. "Been my experience that there comes a time in every man's life when he has to bury the past so he can face the future."

Asher's fingers tightened around his cup. "I'll think about burying the past right after I bury Silas."

Cobb's eyes narrowed. "If you think vengeance will make you feel better, you're a fool, Gabriel."

"It's not about vengeance," said Asher. "It's about justice. It's about tipping the scales back."

"Bullshit. Don't play word games with me, boy. You and I both know the day you put a bullet in Silas' face the only thing that'll be on your mind is revenge. You call it whatever you want so you can sleep better at night, but it won't change the fact that killing Silas is about cold, hard vengeance. Nothing more. And certainly not anything as noble as justice or tipping the damn scales."

"And why shouldn't I have my vengeance?" Asher asked. "I've killed for my country. I've killed for money. So why shouldn't I kill for my own reasons?"

"I never said you wouldn't have your vengeance," Cobb replied. "I just said it won't make you feel any better."

"Only one way to find out."

"Enough," Larissa interjected. "I didn't come all the way out here to listen to you two bicker. Gabriel, we need to get your head stitched up or you'll have one nasty scar."

Asher and Cobb looked at each other across the table. Not in animosity, but mutual respect, each trying to understand the other. Asher knew the old man meant well, but he didn't understand just how deeply Silas had betrayed him. Vengeance was a dark impulse deeply rooted in Asher's soul and he could no more let it go than he could lop off his own leg.

Cobb stood up, went to the sink, and poured the rest of his coffee down the drain. "Well," he said, "I think I'll get out of here and leave you two alone. If you don't mind, I'll take Joe's truck." He chuckled. "Guy loves that Dodge. Maybe I'll tell him I found it dumped in the woods. He'll be so happy to have it back, he'll probably give me a reward. There's a beat-up old Toyota out back if you need it for some reason, but she runs cranky when she's cold."

"Grampy," Larissa protested, "what are you talking about? There's no reason for you to leave."

As usual, Cobb pulled no punches when speaking his mind. "I'm getting out of here for a couple of reasons. For starters, like I said, I need to fetch some groceries, so I can get that business taken care of in the morning. I'm friends with Joe and when I bring him back his beloved truck, he'll let me stay at the motel tonight for nothing, so don't sweat it. But most importantly, unless I'm seriously mistaken—which I usually ain't—I think some time alone would do you two a world of good."

"Matt," Asher said, "it's not like that."

Cobb snorted. "Keep telling yourself that, kid, and maybe one of these days you'll actually start to believe it. Now, where are the keys?"

"Grampy," Larissa said, "you can't be serious."

Asher knew arguing with Cobb was a waste of time once the old man's mind was made up. "Keys are in the ignition. Can I give you some money for groceries?"

"What are you doing, trying to insult me?" Cobb retorted. "You try to give me money and you'll know what it feels like to have a bunch of dead presidents stuffed up your tailpipe." He went over and pecked Larissa on the cheek. "I'll see you in the morning, Lissy. Try not to give Asher too much of a hard time, huh? He's not that bad a guy."

Larissa smiled, apparently resigned to the fact that Cobb was leaving for the night. "Don't worry,

Grampy," she said, giving his hand a squeeze. "I know he's not."

Cobb shrugged into a light jacket and exited the cabin with a final wave. Asher locked the door behind him and watched out the window as Cobb made his way to the Dodge Ram, which started immediately. The headlights punched through the darkness as Cobb deftly executed a three-point turn and began the rumbling journey back down the rocky road. Even here, inside the cabin, Asher noticed how long it took for the sound of the engine to fade from earshot; noise traveled a long way out here in the wild.

He turned away from the window and went into the bedroom, which consisted of two wooden bunks and a dresser with a cracked mirror hanging over it. Both bunks featured foam mattresses but only one had any linen. No surprise there; Cobb hadn't been expecting company.

Asher went back into the other room where Larissa was still sitting by the wood stove, holding her hands out to the warmth. "Find anything interesting?" she asked.

"Found out why your grandfather insisted on leaving."

"Really? Why?"

"There's only two bunks."

"He didn't need to leave just because of that. I think you and I are mature enough to share a bed without making a big deal about it."

"Well, now we each have our own."

"How's your cut?" she asked.

Asher reached up and felt his scalp wound. "Still bleeding a bit. Need to get it cleaned and stitched."

"See if you can find the stuff and I'll patch you up."

Asher found some first-aid supplies in the cupboard above the stove and a sewing kit in the bedroom dresser. Meanwhile, Larissa heated up some water. When it was warm enough, she told him to sit down. She dipped a washcloth in the warm water, wrung it out, used her fingers to locate the cut, and then gently scrubbed away the blood from the gash. She then poured some hydrogen peroxide onto the cloth. "This is going to sting," she warned, pressing it against the cut.

Asher heard the bubbly hiss of the antiseptic doing its work. "Yeah, that smarts."

"That means it's working," Larissa said. "If you think about it, the most painful things in life are also the most cleansing."

Asher grinned. "You sound like a fortune cookie."

"Joke all you want," she said, removing the cloth from his forehead, "but it's true." She felt around until she located the sewing kit and handed it to Asher. "I need you to sterilize the needle and then thread it for me."

There was a box of wooden matches on the table. Asher struck one and it flared to life with a hot hiss. He ran the flame along the length of the needle until he was satisfied it was sterile. He extinguished the match and tossed it in the sink.

Threading the needle turned out to be tougher than he expected. It seemed like the length of thread possessed a mind of its own, an evil mind that stubbornly refused to pass through the eye of the needle. It was worse than trying to cram a cobra through a keyhole. He could field-strip and reassemble an M4 carbine in under forty seconds, but it took him over two minutes to get the needle threaded. His fingers felt clumsy as sausage links. But at last, it was done. "There," he said, handing the threaded needle back to Larissa.

"I thought you were going to take all night," she teased. "A blind man could have done it faster."

She spent the next few minutes working in silence, her movements deft and sure, belying her blindness. She squeezed together the edges of the wound and began sewing it shut. Asher felt the needle sliding in and out of his skin but barely registered the pain. He had been cut by more knives and grazed by more bullets than he cared to remember, so he could shrug off the prick of a needle.

Larissa leaned over to bite off the excess thread. In that instant, Asher felt something pass between them, an invisible but undeniable shift in the air. As Larissa's teeth bit through the thread, her lips grazed his skin and Asher felt her hesitate, lingering for just a moment longer than was necessary. His pulse quickened and heat rushed through his veins. He fought for control as the reins of his emotions began slipping from his grasp. Desire rose up and battered down his resistance, urging him to surrender to the recklessness of the moment.

Larissa's hands came up and softly caressed his face. Her unfocused eyes burned stunningly bright in the warm glow of the gas lamp, sparkling gems that seemed to peer right into his heart. Asher felt breathless but still tried to resist. He reached up and took hold of her wrists. "Larissa, I—"

"Shhhhh." She hushed him as she gently brushed away his hands. "I want to see you."

He knew what she meant, what she wanted. Her

touch was now her eyes, the only "sight" she had left in the aftermath of Macklin's bullet all those years ago. He let his hands fall to his side.

As she leaned in close, Asher could hear the pounding rhythm of her heart. As she gently explored his face, reacquainting herself with the curve of his cheek, the angle of his jaw, the harsh bristle of his facial stubble, Asher tried to convince himself that her touch did nothing for him, but he was just lying to himself. He heard the ragged desire in her breath and knowing how much she wanted him only made Asher want her that much more.

But it was more than just simple carnal urges; it was a yearning for a respite from the darkness. For just a few moments, however fleeting, he didn't want to think about Silas or Macklin or any of his other demons. Tonight, he just wanted to touch and be touched. Tonight, he didn't want to be alone. Tonight, he and Larissa were just two lonely souls with no one else to turn to but each other.

He stood up and pulled her close. She felt good against him, soft and warm and yielding. Her touch made Asher ache with something he had not felt in a long time. Need and desire converged and slammed through him like a bullet, shattering the last vestiges of his hesitation.

His hands slid beneath her shirt, relishing the satin feel of her skin, and her sigh of pleasure became a breathless moan. Her arms glided around his neck, fingers running through his hair as he caressed her.

Asher felt the passion searing away his demons, sloughing them from his soul like an ugly, unwanted skin. Tomorrow they might all come slinking back to sink their venomous fangs in once again, but for now their stranglehold on his heart was broken. He picked Larissa up in his arms, carried her into the bedroom, and laid her down on the bunk.

He undressed her in the dark, the shadows pooling in the secrets of her body. He breathed in the scent of her skin, intoxicated and powerless by the spell weaving through his veins.

He shed his clothes and joined her on the bed, naked flesh sliding together with the satiny friction of skin on skin. Larissa drew his face down to hers, her lips every bit as soft and sweet as Asher remembered. He melted into her, lost in the moment. She clutched him tight as her mouth flowered open beneath his hungry kiss, their tongues writhing together in hot, sensual abandon.

They surrendered to each other completely, wholly, without reservation. Larissa gasped as Asher began to lose control, his body moving with hers in urgent rhythms, mutual ecstasy burning them both to the breaking point. Moments later they were rocked to their very core as they succumbed to the all-consuming rush of release.

After, they lay curled together in a tangle of limbs. Asher looked at her and saw sweat on her face. No, wait, not sweat—tears. "Hey," he said. "What's wrong?"

She brushed away the tears. "Nothing."

"Tell me."

She took his hand, fingers interlaced, quiet for a long time before she spoke. "I love you, Gabriel. More than you can ever know."

He squeezed her hand but said nothing.

Fresh tears glistened in her eyes. "You can't say it, can you?" It wasn't really a question.

Asher opened his mouth to speak, but then closed it. He could not say what she wanted to hear and anything else would be woefully inadequate.

"I don't understand." Her voice was a whisper in the dark. "After all these years, what are the odds I would be in the apartment right next door to a bunch of mercenaries you were hunting? Have you even thought about what that means?"

"It was just a coincidence." Rain began to patter on the roof. Droplets streamed down the window.

"You can call it coincidence if that makes it easier for you," she said. "But you and I both know that it was something more. Call it fate, call it God, call it destiny, but we were meant to find each other again."

He pulled her close and looked into her blinded eyes. "You might be right," he said softly. "But right now, this is all I have to give."

She smiled up at him through her tears. "If all we have is tonight, then I want to make it a night I'll never forget."

They made love again, the fierceness of the first time now replaced by tenderness. Shadows writhed on the walls and rain danced on the roof as they lost themselves in each other. Asher could feel his demons knocking on the door of his soul, but he refused to let them in. Not tonight. Tonight was for peace, however brief. Tonight, he was not an assassin; no, tonight, he was normal and as he made love to Larissa, he longed for the normalcy to last more than just a few hours. He craved a life free of bullets and blood.

She's offered it to you, an inner voice said. *Why don't you take it?*

I can't.

Can't...or won't?

He didn't know the answer to that.

Would there ever come a time when his hands did something other than kill? Would he even know how to live that kind of life? Probably not, truth be told. Live by the gun, die by the gun. That was his existence. Anything else seemed like a pipe dream.

And then he stopped thinking about anything other than being with Larissa. As they surrendered to each other over and over again through the long, sweet hours of the night, he did his best to ignore the feeling that the stitches in his heart had started to fray.

CHAPTER 14

AFTER LEAVING Asher and Larissa at the cabin, it took Cobb less than thirty minutes to drive to Joe's Motel, but by the time he got there his bladder was begging for relief. It was that damned road. All that bumping and bouncing played havoc with a man's innards. He should have just pulled over and watered the weeds but the thought of exiting the truck's toasty warmth for the cold of the night had convinced him he could hold it until he got to Joe's.

Nobody manned the counter, so Cobb banged on a rusty silver bell for service. He had to bang it again and again until Joe appeared, taking so long that Cobb was tempted to piss right there on the damn floor. But despite hurling a litany of curses, the motel owner gave him a room free of charge when he found out Cobb had returned his precious truck.

"Just remember," Joe said, "no orgies in the room."

"Yeah, yeah, I know. Unless you're invited."

"You betcha."

Even though his bladder was threatening to go

ballistic on him, Cobb took a moment to examine the bullet-riddled Jeep out back. He whistled to himself when he saw the damage done by the chopper's .50 caliber machinegun. Asher and Larissa were lucky to be alive. Well, if you could call two people being hunted by a Company kill-squad "lucky".

He found his room and hurried to the toilet. The bathroom was not much bigger than a broom closet and the light flickered with a sputtering noise, but Cobb didn't care. He took care of business and decided that happiness was an empty bladder.

Cobb washed up and went back out into his motel room. Not much to look at, but it was clean. He wondered how things were going back at his cabin. It was pretty obvious that Larissa's old feelings for Asher were back. Or more likely, had never left in the first place. Cobb fervently hoped Asher wouldn't break her heart all over again, because a broken heart had put those scars on her wrists and Cobb never wanted to go through those dark days again.

He considered turning on the TV, but decided it was late and he needed to get some sleep. Not that he was tired. The unusual events and unfamiliar surroundings sucked the slumber right out of him as if he had mainlined 400 milligrams of caffeine. Still, he had to try, or he would be a zombie in the morning.

He crawled into bed and laid there wide awake for what seemed like forever. He didn't regret giving up his cabin to Asher and Larissa, but right now he craved the warm familiarity of his own bunk.

He stared up at the ceiling and reflected on the story Asher had relayed to him. Sounded like that boy was eyeball-deep in shit and the only way out was to suck it up. This Macklin hombre seemed like a particularly nasty demon and Cobb knew all too well that some demons took a lot of killing before they went down for good. And if Asher's old pal Silas was still breathing, then that meant Asher was walking around with two bullseyes painted on his back. Cobb hoped for Asher's sake—not to mention Larissa's—that Silas was dead and sucking on the devil's knob right about now.

Cobb felt the darkness of depressing thoughts weighing down on him. He was hardly a prayer warrior, but he fired one off anyway. Never hurt to hedge your bets.

Praying made him think about God, which in turn made him grab his mortality by the scruff of the neck and stare it in the face. He was an old man, no denying that, and death waited just around the corner. But the thought of dying didn't really bother him, even though he wasn't really sure what waited on the other side. Heaven? Hell? Disneyland? When it came right down to the nitty-gritty, nobody knew for sure until their time came.

No, it wasn't dying itself that scared him, but dying *shamefully*. As cliché as it sounded, he wanted to die like a man. He wanted to spit in the Grim Reaper's eye and tell him to shove that sickle right up his bony backside.

Asher would die well when his turn came, of that Cobb had no doubt. And his turn might very well come while protecting Larissa. The irony was not lost on Cobb; in order to protect his beloved granddaughter from killers, he had entrusted her into the hands of a killer. But there was nobody Cobb would rather have as Larissa's guardian in these dangerous circumstances.

Asher would die to defend her, would give his life for hers if necessary. As far as Cobb was concerned, that made up for a whole lot of shortcomings.

He hastily fired off another prayer. He didn't know if it got any further than the ceiling, but it made him feel better, and maybe that was the point.

Please, God, don't let him die. You already took Todd away from Larissa; don't take Asher too. Besides, I'm sure You know that this Colonel Macklin fella needs to die, so why don't You do us all a big favor and let Asher cram a .45 down the motherfucker's throat and make him eat a bullet.

Not a pretty prayer, but Cobb figured God got the point.

———

When Cobb awoke a few hours later, he instantly sensed that something was wrong. He had slept badly, tossing and turning on the unfamiliar bed. The sheets were tangled in sweaty knots around his legs and feet, which felt hot and clammy. But the sensation he felt was not one of discomfort, but one of menace. Everything was too quiet, too hushed, as if the world had just shut up. An unnatural silence that Cobb didn't like, not one bit.

Thin gray light seeped through a gap in the window blinds, letting him know dawn had arrived. But that uneasy feeling continued to churn his guts. He listened for a sound, any sound, in the semi-darkness of the room. But all he heard was his breath rattling in his throat and the too-fast beat of his old ticker. Panic hit him for a moment—maybe he was having a heart attack.

No, wait, that couldn't be it; he didn't feel any pain in his chest.

He took several deep breaths, forcing his heart to slow down. It finally did, but the uneasy feeling still clung to him like a second skin. He had to get back to Larissa and Asher right now. Something was wrong. He could feel it.

He hurried into the bathroom, splashed some cold water on his face, then got dressed and opened the door.

He never heard the shot that took him just above his belt buckle. Just felt the blow of the bullet blasting through him, the burning pain of things inside him being torn apart. The impact flung him backward as if struck by the hand of God and he landed in a sitting position slumped against the side of the bed. When he clasped his hands over his belly, something that reminded him of hot maple syrup spilled over his fingers, which suddenly began to shake.

Oh God, I've been shot!

He tried to stand up, but the agony forced him back down with a strangled cry. Whatever he faced next, he would have to face on the floor. The thought left a bitter taste in his mouth, worse even than the pain that now gnawed on every nerve.

He looked at the open door, a rectangle of gray light. For just a second, he could see a black, military-style Hummer parked outside, then a hulking figure filled the doorway, nothing but a silhouette.

Though Cob couldn't make out his features, he could certainly make out the pistol in the man's hand. Looked like a Glock with a suppressor, which explained why he hadn't heard the shot that drilled him.

The silhouetted man didn't speak. Just stood there,

exuding menace. Finally, he reached for the light switch and in the sudden illumination, Cobb saw the savage scar stretched across his throat like a shiny grin. "Macklin," Cobb said through pain-clenched teeth. "You bastard."

Macklin stepped into the room and closed the door. To Cobb, it sounded like a coffin lid clicking shut. He knew he didn't have any chance of leaving this room alive.

I'll never see Larissa again.

Tears burned his eyes, but he refused to let them fall. Macklin would take pleasure in them and Cobb refused to give the sick psychopath anything to smile about. Instead, he steeled himself for what would come next.

Macklin holstered the Glock and crouched down in front of him. His frigid gaze scrutinized Cobb like a viper sizing up its next victim. "Looks like you were in the wrong place at the wrong time, Mr. Cobb." Macklin's voice was a barely intelligible rasp.

Cobb started to reply but got interrupted by a coughing fit that left his lips spackled with blood. "So you know who I am," he finally managed to say.

"After we tracked Asher's Jeep to this location, we naturally had some questions, and your friend Joe was nice enough to tell us about his stolen truck and the fact that you brought it back. Eventually, he told us all about you. Took a little persuasion, but that's something at which I excel. Once he gave up your name—and room number, obviously—I just ran you through the Company databanks and now I know pretty much everything there is to know about you."

"Just like God, huh?"

"Pretty close."

Another blood-flecked coughing fit gripped Cobb. Good Lord, he was messed up bad. "If you're God," he said when he could speak again, "I think I'd rather suck the devil's dick."

Macklin smiled thinly. "You've got balls, old man, I'll give you that."

"You've got balls too," Cobb said, "and if you don't mind, I'd like to chop the suckers off and hang them from my rearview mirror. I think they'd make a pearl of a conversation piece."

Macklin chuckled, a cold sound without mirth. "Let me lay out the situation for you." He pointed at Cobb's wound. "You've been gut shot and you're going to die. Unfortunately, gut shots are notoriously slow, and you'll probably live for at least another three hours and those hours will be spent in excruciating agony. That's the bad news."

Cobb was feeling some of that excruciating agony right now. Sweat beaded on his forehead. "Thanks for putting such a rosy spin on things. Now why don't you get to the point before those three hours are up?"

Macklin retained his cruel, razored smile. "The point is," he said, "there's also some good news, and the good news is, if you tell me where Asher and your granddaughter are holed up, I'll give you a quick death. How's that for a reasonable offer?"

"I've got a better one," Cobb countered. "You tell me what I want to know and then I'll tell you what you want to know."

Macklin's features were so stone-faced inscrutable they deserved a place on Mt. Rushmore. "All depends on what you want to know."

"Like it matters," said Cobb. "I'm a dead man no matter what. You could tell me who really killed JFK and it wouldn't make any difference. But all I really want to know is how you found the Jeep here."

"There's an electro-magnetic tracking device attached to the frame of the Jeep and linked to a Company satellite, so I always know where Asher is, as long as he uses the Jeep. But now the Jeep is here, and Asher is not and quite frankly, that pisses me off. So do yourself a favor and tell me where he is."

"One more question," Cobb said. "When did you put the tracker on the Jeep?"

"I sent a couple of protégés to his house a few days ago. They attached the device before they initiated the strike and got themselves killed. Now I've answered your questions, so it's your turn to answer mine—where are they?"

"Yeah, uh, I sort of lied when I said I would answer your questions. You can go to hell."

"Fine, we'll do this the hard way." Macklin yanked Cobb to his feet and threw him on the bed. Cobb landed in a pile of blood and pain, his savaged guts wrenching a terrible cry past his lips. Those lips turned to pulp when Macklin smashed the cry back down his throat with a brutal backhand.

Using plastic flex cuffs, Macklin bound Cobb's hands and feet and then used a knife to cut away his clothes. The old man endured the indignities in silence. On his best day he was no match for Macklin's strength, let alone a day like this, with a hole in his stomach where his navel used to be. Blood loss had shocked his system far beyond the point of any resistance. He was utterly at Macklin's mercy and Cobb was pretty sure the man didn't even know the meaning of the word.

Macklin gagged him, pulled on a pair of latex gloves, and went to work with methodical, surgical precision, submerging Cobb in a hell of agony beyond anything he could have fathomed. Still, it took nearly an hour to break him and before Macklin pulled the information from his bleeding body and past his mashed lips, one-third of his skin, eight teeth, six fingers, four toes, and one testicle lay in a messy pile next to him.

Macklin removed his dripping gloves. "All you had to do was tell me what I wanted to know, but you wanted to play hard. Well, was that hard enough for you, old man?"

Cobb lay in a dark world of blood and pain. He felt death creeping closer and welcomed it. His swollen lips moved, pleading for an end to the agony. But Macklin just stared at him with dead eyes, drinking in Cobb's pain as if it were the elixir on which his soul thrived.

Even through the pain afflicting every molecule of his being, Cobb felt an acute sense of failure. He had broken, had told Macklin where to find Larissa and Asher. The betrayal burned like bitter bile deep down inside him. He not only *wanted* to die, he *deserved* to die for what he had done.

Cobb nearly sobbed in desperate relief when the pistol appeared in Macklin's hands. Here, at last, was the end. "You've been very helpful, old man," Macklin said. "Must sting, knowing you helped kill your own granddaughter, but I want you to know I appreciate it."

The pistol rose, slowly, and Cobb followed its rising trajectory until it came to a stop. The black hole at the end of the suppressor stared at him with hypnotic, unwavering intensity, and then Macklin pulled the trigger. There was no pain, just the heavy impact of the bullet hitting him between the eyes. In his last slivered nanosecond of life, he had only one final thought.

Forgive me, Larissa.

And then he was gone.

CHAPTER 15

WHEN ASHER AWOKE SHORTLY after dawn, he didn't move; just laid very still, listening to the sounds of the cabin and the surrounding woods, using his fine-tuned instincts to probe for any hint of threat. He did it automatically, no conscious thought, the process as natural to him as breathing.

Rain no longer rapped on the roof, but droplets dappled the window, so the showers had stopped shortly before he woke up. Outside, raindrops would be clinging to the leaves and the woods would be hushed, the kind of quiet found only in nature.

Beside him, Larissa stirred, caught in that no-man's-land between sleep and wakefulness, one arm draped across his chest. Their lovemaking last night had been both fierce and gentle and left his self-control shattered. Even now, looking at her as she curled peacefully against him, he felt the desire to once again surrender to what lay between them.

Larissa's eyes flickered open. For just a moment, Asher imagined she was looking at him. But of course, that was impossible. She stretched languidly, like a cat, and murmured, "What time is it?"

"Not sure," Asher said. He had removed his watch when things heated up last night and now had no idea where it was. Probably lying on the floor with the rest of his clothes. "Judging from the light coming through yonder window, I'd say it's about an hour past dawn."

"Did you just say 'yonder'?" Her eyes sparkled with amusement.

"Yeah, so?"

"Pretty poetic word for a guy like you."

"I have my moments."

"Yes, you do." She pressed close to him. "And I wish this moment could last forever."

"Larissa..."

She reached up and touched a finger to his lips. "Don't say it. I know, okay? I know. But that doesn't change how I feel."

"I'm sorry."

"That doesn't change anything either."

Asher had no response to that.

Larissa was quiet for several moments, finger tracing the ridge of his collarbone. Finally, she said, "Penny for your thoughts?"

"They're not worth that much."

"Tell me anyway."

"Some other time."

"Do you promise me there will be some other time?" she asked softly.

Asher recognized that this was a pivotal moment, an opportunity to open his heart, share the emotions bottled up inside him and maybe change the course of his life. All he had to do was say the words she wanted to hear.

But instead, he said, "I can't make a promise I'm not sure I can keep."

The moment withered away and crawled back into its dark hole, maybe never to surface again. How many times can you crush hope before it finally dies? Asher suspected he would find out before his life ended. Which would be sooner rather than later if Macklin or Silas had their way.

Asher's anger slow burned inside him, simmering like hot coals. He was sick of walking around with crosshairs on his back, wondering when the bullet with his name would strike.

Larissa moved beside him. "Hey, are you sure you're all right?"

He heard the concern in her voice, the love she felt for him. As much as he longed to reciprocate, he knew he could not share his life with her because it might very well get her killed, just like Karen. He could not bear the thought of another innocent dying because of him.

An image of a wind-swept grave with his wife's name etched in the stone appeared in his mind and his lips tightened in a grim line.

"Gabriel?" Larissa reached up and touched his face.

"I'm fine," he said. "Just thinking about Karen."

Hurt flickered across her face, there one moment, gone the next. "I'm sorry," she said.

"Don't be sorry. You didn't kill her."

"Neither did you."

"In a way, yes, I did."

"You don't really believe that do you?"

Asher didn't answer. Only the beating of their hearts broke the silence. It was a silence made for grim thoughts and Asher obliged by thinking of his murdered wife and Larissa's murdered husband, each felled by Macklin's blade and bullets. Asher looked down at Larissa. They shared the same wounds.

But she had survived, refusing to let life twist her into a bitter shell. She had rolled with the punches, accepted her pain, and moved on. Tried by fire, she had emerged from the flames stronger than before, a beautiful blend of silk and steel. Asher knew he paled in comparison. He used anger as a shield and bitterness as armor. He might be better at the killing game, but Larissa was the better person.

He slid out of bed and opened the window, feeling the brisk morning air on his skin. Outside, ground fog clung to the earth in an unbroken marsh of mist, smothering everything in a gray shroud that would endure until the rising sun burned it away. Bare branches groped through the fog's surface like the fleshless fingers of long-dead corpses struggling to rise from their soupy graves.

Asher looked up at the streaks of sky visible through the canopy of branches. It was clear and growing lighter by the minute. Soon the sun would show its face, the fog would fade away, Cobb would return, and hopefully they could spend the day in relative peace, safe from their hunters, at least for now.

Asher left the window open as he dressed, listening to the birdsong outside. Now that dawn was here, the woods were coming alive.

Larissa smiled from the bed. "You always were an early riser."

Asher slipped on his shoulder rig, checked the .45 to ensure a bullet nestled in the pipe, and then slid the gun into its holster. "Some things never change."

"You don't have to remind me of that."

Asher glanced at her but before he could respond, he heard the sound of an approaching engine. Still some distance down the road but getting closer.

"Sounds like Grampy's back," Larissa said.

Asher almost agreed, but then the sound separated into plural components. Not one engine, but two. The blood chilled in his veins. "That's not Grampy."

Larissa sat up in bed, spurred by his sudden tension. "Talon?"

"Either that or some very determined Jehovah's Witnesses." He picked her clothes up off the floor and handed them to her. "Get dressed. We have to get out of here."

Larissa began pulling on her clothes as fast as she could. Meanwhile, Asher rigged the cabin door with enough C-4 to reduce the place to toothpicks. The first unlucky Talon operative to breach the cabin would be in for one nasty surprise.

Knock-knock. Bang-bang. Bye-bye.

By the time he finished setting the charges, the rumble of engines was very close. Moving quickly, he helped Larissa out the open window in the back room, then grabbed the duffel bag and crawled out after her.

Grabbing her hand, he led her into the evergreen thicket on the other side of the road. Their breath plumed in the cold morning air. Frosted leaves, hidden by the ground fog, crunched under their feet. Once in the thicket, they hugged the earth, using the soupy mist for concealment, and waited for Talon to arrive. Asher checked the shotgun, making sure it was loaded to capacity. If Macklin gave him an opening, Asher planned on taking the bastard out.

The rumble of engines evolved into a full-throated roar. Two Hummers lumbered into sight, dirt spewing from their knobby, oversized tires. Macklin rode shotgun in the lead vehicle and Asher felt a rush of rage hot enough to melt bone to ash. His finger curled around the SPAS-12's trigger but he knew he couldn't take the shot. Military-grade Hummers meant heavy armoring and bullet-resistant glass. If he fired at Macklin now, the buckshot would just ricochet off the windshield and leave their position exposed. A pointless, inexcusable tactical mistake. So he put a leash on his rage and took his finger off the trigger.

The sky lightened above them, dawn yielding to day. The fog felt cold and clammy on his skin. Larissa knelt beside him, hugging herself for warmth. Asher's eyes softened when he looked at her. Then, as if someone had flicked a switch, they hardened again as he turned back toward Black Talon. They were the eyes of vengeance and revealed the primal forces contained in Asher's heart.

The Hummers halted almost directly in front of them, the roar of their monstrous 6.5-liter V-8 engines aggressively loud and out of place in the serenity of the forest. A moment later, the drivers killed the motors, and Macklin and the five remaining members of Black Talon exited the vehicles. Asher fixed his gaze on the man who had murdered his wife and felt his pulse quicken with fury.

Using the Hummers as shields between themselves and the cabin, Macklin and his operatives braced their

Colt M4A1 carbines across the hoods, roofs, and bumpers. The woods seemed to have gone absurdly quiet. The fog slithered like a living entity, suffusing the scene with surrealistic stillness. Nature itself seemed to hold its breath. A dead leaf fell from a nearby oak, and Asher imagined he could actually hear the sound of the stem breaking away from the branch. His eyes followed the leaf as it floated toward the ground.

And then the silence was shattered.

"*FIRE!*" Macklin roared with his mangled voice, slamming back his trigger.

Six rifles blazed in unison, singing a high-powered hell-song.

Crouched in the fog, Asher watched the 5.56mm bullets pound the cabin. The wave of lead tore hundreds of holes in the walls and exploded the windows as Talon raked the place from floor to rafters. Asher smiled coldly. It was overkill and revealed to Asher just how dangerous Macklin considered him to be. Flattery by firepower, damn straight.

The magazines in the M4s emptied in a matter of seconds. Silence returned and burnt gunpowder left a bite in the air. Spent brass littered the vehicles. In the fog beside him, Larissa remained as still as humanly possible.

Macklin motioned for one of his Talon soldiers to check the cabin.

The man dropped into a combat crouch and hustled over the misty terrain until he hugged the cabin wall, then cautiously edged toward the porch. The air was so still that even from fifty yards away, Asher could hear the shattered glass crunching under the operator's boots. He watched with grim anticipation as the man ascended the rickety steps and kicked open the door.

The cabin erupted in a massive, disintegrating blast. The roof lurched into the sky, riding a mushroom cloud of roiling flame. The walls burst apart and sprayed sharp fragments of wood in all directions like shrapnel, turning the Talon soldier into human confetti.

Macklin and his remaining operatives ducked for cover behind the Hummers as burning debris washed over them. A flaming board bounced off a windshield in a splash of sparks. A Talon gunner crumpled to the ground with a sword-sized shard of wood skewering his throat. More high-velocity wood slivers ripped open another man's leg, slashing his femoral artery in three different places and guaranteeing a quick demise.

From his concealment, Asher watched Macklin climb to his feet, dripping with mud. If the man were smart, he would retreat, withdraw the few troops he had left, and reorganize for another assault at a later time.

But Asher had no intention of letting that happen.

It ends today. Right here, right now.

With Macklin positioned on the far side of the Hummer, Asher didn't have the proper angle to kill his nemesis just yet. But he could damn sure keep him from getting away.

Asher raised the shotgun. Fog fell from the barrel like an unwanted veil. He pressed it to his shoulder and aimed low.

Focused on the fiery ruin of the cabin and his dying men, Macklin never sensed the danger lurking in the fog behind him.

Asher hit the trigger twice in rapid succession.

The buckshot whipped under the Hummer and chopped into Macklin's exposed boots.

The blasts shredded through his calves and ankles and literally blew his feet off. Macklin went down, snarling in sudden pain, but managed to pull himself behind the front tire and out of the line of fire. Asher glimpsed a mess of torn flesh and splintered bone where Macklin's lower legs should have been. Unless he could walk on his bloody stumps, Macklin wasn't going anywhere.

His enemy hobbled by a twelve-gauge double amputation, Asher turned his attention to the remaining two Talon commandos.

Both were on Asher's side of the Hummers. Neither knew Asher's location because he was crouched down low in the fog. This lack of knowledge meant they could not take evasive action; in order to move away from a threat, one must know where the threat is. So they simply knelt down beside the vehicles and scanned the woods, peering over assault rifles tucked tight to their shoulders, seeking target acquisition.

They quickly found out *they* were the targets and they had already been acquired.

Asher triggered two quick shots from the SPAS-12. The first operative took the brunt of the blast right below the eyebrows and went somersaulting backward with the top half of his head blown to pulp.

The second Talon soldier caught a dose of buckshot low in his torso. The sledgehammer force folded him in half, and he flopped face-down in the muck.

Smoke twisted in ghostly curls from the barrel of the shotgun as Asher stood up, watching the two bodies twitch spastically. Black Talon was decimated, gutted, a total loss. Time to put down the mad dog they called master.

"Wait here," Asher said to Larissa.

"Where are you going?"

"To finish this."

He edged cautiously toward the Hummer behind which Macklin sat, badly wounded. But even badly wounded, Asher knew better than to underestimate Macklin. The man had survived having his throat cut. It would take more than losing his feet to rob him of his lethality.

As he crossed the pungent, swampy earth, Asher saw a shape moving inside the cab of the Hummer and realized that Macklin had crawled in. Asher closed the gap as fast as he could, but Macklin managed to slam the door shut and hit the locks, securing himself inside a shell of armor plating and ballistic glass.

Asher stood outside and glared at him. He thought about venting his frustration by emptying the SPAS-12 into the windshield. No glass is truly bulletproof and multiple rounds from the shotgun would eventually break through. But Asher had a better idea, one that didn't eat up his ammunition.

Inside the Hummer, Macklin ripped strips from his shirt and fashioned tourniquets which he tied around both thighs to keep himself from bleeding out. When he finished, he leaned back in the passenger seat, face an unhealthy shade of white, but smiling his cruel, razor-slash of a grin. "So close, Asher, and yet so far."

"You're acting like the game is over," Asher said. "From where I'm standing, looks like checkmate, asshole."

"I've stopped the bleeding, so all I have to do now is call for backup and then sit here and wait. You say I've lost the game, I say I'm just pausing."

Asher smiled coldly. "Hold that thought."

He walked back over to Larissa and pulled a brick of C-4 out of his duffel bag.

"Is it over?" she asked.

"Almost," Asher said. "Just need to burn the snake out of his hole."

He walked back over to the Hummer and slapped the explosive onto the windshield right in front of Macklin's face.

Macklin's grin faded and for a moment, true fear stained his eyes. But he recovered quickly. "Go ahead," he taunted. "I'd rather be blown to bits than come out there and let you get your hands on me."

"Then sit there and burn." Asher set the detonator for twenty seconds. "I'm good with that."

He plunged the detonator into the C-4, then ducked behind a tree outside the blast radius and yelled, "Larissa, keep your head down!" He peered around the trunk just enough to lock eyes with Macklin through the windshield as the numbers ran down toward zero.

Macklin held fast and defiant until just five seconds remained. Then his survival instincts kicked into high gear. He scrambled to open the door and threw himself out as the final second expired.

The explosion tore the Hummer apart.

The fiery blast picked Macklin up in midair like a giant fist and hurled him into a nearby tree. He smashed into it with his back and his body folded around the trunk at an unnatural angle, like a piece of cooked spaghetti thrown against a fence post. Even over the crackle of flames, Asher heard the sharp crack of Macklin's spine snapping in two.

Asher found the Talon leader lying broken and paralyzed at the foot of the tree. The blast had scorched off most of his hair and his clothes smoldered. He stared up at Asher with eyes that begged for death.

Asher was happy to oblige.

He pulled out his dagger and crouched down in front of Macklin. Without hesitation, he drove the blade hilt-deep into the side of Macklin's neck, at the exact point where the ghastly scar began. "This is for my wife, you son of a bitch," he rasped, then slashed the knife all the way through Macklin's throat, following the path of the scar, cutting carotids, jugular, and windpipe in one savage stroke. "This time you die for real." Blood geysered from the gaping wound.

Asher ignored the splatter and stared into Macklin's eyes as he died. It was finally over. The man who had murdered his wife, gunned down Larissa's husband, put a bullet in her head, and blinded her for life, was finally dead.

He stood up and headed back to the other side of the road where Larissa waited. As he rounded the rear of the burning Hummer, he walked past the fallen body of the Talon operative he had shotgunned low in the torso. With his attention focused on getting back to Larissa, he never saw the operative—whom he had believed to be dead—raise the M4 with a trembling hand.

His first hint of danger was a triple burst of auto fire from behind him. All three slugs flew wide due to the gunner's unsteady hand, but not by much. They slammed into a tree to Asher's left, carving away splinters and fragments.

He reacted instantly, rolling to his right behind another tree, using it to shield himself from the Talon soldier. He desperately looked for Larissa.

She was right where he had left her, hidden in the fog, just her head visible through the thin wisps that formed the top layer of the mist. As he spotted her, she cried out, "Gabriel!"

The Talon gunner fired in the direction of her voice, spraying the fog with bullets.

Asher heard the telltale slap of lead against flesh and saw Larissa's head jerk to the side. Icy fingers reached into his chest and gripped his heart as he saw blood cascading down her face. She slumped into the mud as the fog turned crimson.

No! Asher screamed silently, the words trapped in his constricted throat. *Not again!*

He raised the SPAS-12, Larissa's blood-drenched face driving him to kill. The shotgun roared again and again and again, smashing apart the man's chest, shredding his heart and lungs.

Threat neutralized, Asher ran to Larissa and felt for a pulse. It was weak and fluttery, but it was there. She was alive, but God only knew for how long. Blood darkened the left side of her face. He had to get her to a hospital.

His breath plumed in the autumn air and he trembled, not from the cold, but from the thought of losing her. *Please, God, don't let her die on me.*

He cradled her head in his lap and tried to wipe away the blood, but there was too much of it, making it impossible to tell how much damage the bullet had done. He ripped off two strips from his shirt. He folded one into a makeshift bandage, covered the wound, then used the other strip to tie around Larissa's head and hold the bandage in place.

He carried her to the second Hummer and strapped her into the passenger seat. As he climbed behind the wheel, Asher heard the crackle and pop of flames as the cabin continued to burn. He turned the key and the Hummer rumbled to life. Asher maneuvered the vehicle around in a tight U-turn, crunching Macklin's corpse under the oversized tires as he did so and not giving a damn.

He resisted the urge to gun the gas. The path was rough enough as it was; high speed would only intensify the bouncing and jarring and might do more damage to Larissa's head wound.

Assuming she's alive at all.

Asher crushed that thought before the barbs could sink in.

Time crawled. The trail seemed to go on forever. But dirt finally turned to blacktop, and Asher punched it, rubber howling in protest. He wiped the sweat from his brow and cracked a window to let in some air. Wind rushed into the cab and Asher felt something brush against his arm. He glanced down. It was Larissa's hair, the silken strands sodden with blood, red on gold.

Guts churning, he drove faster.

CHAPTER 16

WITH THE PEDAL PINNED, it took Asher less than twenty minutes to reach Glens Falls Hospital. Larissa slumped in the seat, held up only by her safety belt. Asher kept thinking she had died, but when he placed his fingers against her neck, he could feel a weak pulse. She was a fighter who had cheated death once. Asher prayed she could do it again.

He pulled up to the Emergency entrance and exited the vehicle. He left the SPAS-12 in the Hummer, keeping only the HK45 pistol. He quickly unfastened Larissa from the seatbelt and lifted her out of the cab. She hung in his arms like a rag doll, head lolling limply on her neck.

The automatic doors opened with a pneumatic hiss as he carried her inside. Blood dripped from the now-sodden makeshift bandage, the droplets absurdly red under the bright lights, as if they belonged in some abstract painting. Asher felt fear and panic gnawing away at him as he headed for a set of double doors in front of him.

A nurse darted out from behind a desk, her eyes sizing up Asher and the bloody bundle in his arms. "What happened to her?"

"She's been shot in the head."

"This way."

Asher followed her through the double doors into a long corridor. The nurse led him into the first room on the right and pointed to the examination table. Asher laid Larissa down, careful not to jostle her head. The room smelled of antiseptic.

The nurse snatched the phone from the wall. "Get Dr. Morrow down here now!" she said to whoever was on the other end of the line. "I've got a Code Two GSW in Trauma One."

Asher kept looking at Larissa. Even now, covered with blood, she was beautiful. He should have told her that. He should have told her a lot of things. And now it looked like he might never get another chance.

A doctor burst into the room, stethoscope flapping around his neck. The nametag clipped to his white coat identified him as Dr. Morrow, a short man with a receding hairline, gentle eyes, and the slender fingers of a surgeon. "Status report," he said to the nurse as he started toward Larissa. But he hesitated when he glimpsed the gun under Asher's duster. He eyed the assassin warily, giving him the kind of look usually reserved for strange dogs when you don't know whether to believe the wagging tail or the bared teeth.

"Please," Asher said. "Help her."

"I want to," said Morrow. "But the gun..."

"Is no threat to you. You have my word on that."

Morrow didn't look fully convinced, but he buckled down to business. As he peeled off the bandage, he said to the nurse, "Get me some help in here, stat." When he dropped the bandage into a stainless-steel basin, it made a disturbingly soggy splat sound that reeked of finality. Morrow pulled the overhead light down for a closer inspection of Larissa's wound as the nurse called for assistance.

Asher felt utterly helpless. He wanted to beg, plead, say something, anything, to let Morrow know just how desperate he was for Larissa to survive. But they were beyond words at this point. Morrow would do his job and Larissa would either live or die. It was as simple as that.

He knew he couldn't stay with her, as much as he wanted to. The police would be summoned soon if they hadn't already. Standard hospital procedure for gunshot wounds. He leaned over Larissa's lifeless form and whispered, "I'll be back," knowing she couldn't hear him but needing to tell her anyway.

Footsteps pounded in the corridor outside. The door flew open and what seemed like a mob of hospital personnel poured in. Asher slipped out of the room as people scurried this way and that, players in an orchestra of organized chaos designed to pull Larissa back from the brink.

Out in the hallway, Asher leaned against the wall and tried to compose himself. His emotions floated randomly through his heart and soul, jagged fragments unable or unwilling to come together and form a cohesive picture. He wanted to go back into the room, wanted to stay with Larissa as she fought for her very life. But he knew he couldn't. If he stayed here, he would be taken into custody when the police arrived, and he would be no good to Larissa behind bars.

Besides, there was something he needed to do. Something he should have done a long time ago.

He walked away before he could change his mind. With every step further away from Larissa, his conscience punished him, accused him of abandoning her when she needed him most. But he kept walking because he had no other choice.

Outside, clouds thickened the sky, and a light drizzle spattered the windshield like tears as Asher got into the Hummer and drove away.

CHAPTER 17

AS HE DROVE out of the hospital parking lot, Asher saw police cruisers approaching. Their pulsating lights painted a surrealistic red and blue montage on his windshield, the colors smeared by the rain. Asher tensed; if anyone had told the cops that he was driving a Hummer, it was game over. The early stages of a headache pounded on his temples as the wipers flicked back and forth in a hypnotic rhythm.

The police flashed by and Asher saw by the markings on the cars that they were city boys. Either nobody had called the State Police yet or they were just lagging behind. Either way, he didn't intend to stick around to find out. He merged with traffic and made his way out of the city.

He stopped at a used car lot that hadn't opened yet, ditching the Hummer in favor of a nondescript Ford Ranger 4x4. He quickly hot-wired the truck and got back on the road. The Ranger was badly out of alignment and the interior smelled like moldy gym socks, but it ran.

Asher turned on the wipers, sluicing away the rain, and listened to the tires hiss over the wet road in a vain attempt to take his mind off Larissa. With every passing mile, it became harder and harder not to turn around and go back. Not knowing if she was alive or dead gnawed at his guts.

He was so distracted that he failed to notice the black Toyota Tacoma tailing him, his combat instincts dulled by his troubled heart. The Toyota stayed several cars back as Asher drove through town, following in his wake like a disembodied shadow, just one vehicle amidst many.

Asher turned onto Route 196 and started driving across what the locals called the Flats, a two-mile, arrow-straight stretch of road with nothing on either side except old barns, crop fields, and barbed wire fences. Glancing in the rearview mirror, he saw the black Tacoma about a hundred yards back but paid it no mind. Route 196 was the main connection between Hudson Falls and Hartford and saw more traffic than one might think, considering it was just a two-lane country road.

The next time he looked in the rearview, the Tacoma completely filled it. A second later the truck rammed him, metal crunching on metal.

At 60 mph, the impact nearly sent Asher sailing off the road. He fought the Ford for control, cursing through clenched teeth as the back end fishtailed wildly. For one breathless instant, he was sure he was going to nosedive into the ditch at terminal velocity. He wrenched at the wheel, straining to keep the Ranger on the road. The tires suddenly found their grip again, biting into the shoulder. Asher whipped back onto the pavement, dirt and stones spraying everywhere.

The Tacoma pulled up alongside the Ford. Asher glanced over and saw the spurting flame of a muzzle flash. The window exploded over him in a wave of glass. He felt the bullet sizzle past the tip of his nose before blowing out the opposite window. Wind and rain howled into the cab, cold and stinging.

He stomped the brakes, bringing the Ford to a rubber-screeching halt. The Tacoma rocketed past him. Asher throttled the steering wheel like it was the throat of the driver who was trying to kill him. Anger and adrenalin pumped through his veins.

Up ahead, the Tacoma executed a skidding 180-degree turn so that it faced Asher. They looked like two rivals preparing to play a game of chicken. Asher locked onto the face of the driver and a jolt ran through him.

Silas.

Asher didn't waste time trying to figure out how Silas had found him, because it didn't matter. Some force in the universe—destiny, fate, God—seemed hell-bent on playing havoc with his life this week. The machinations behind the moments were irrelevant.

Asher stared at his former best friend and Silas stared back, dark emotions bridging the gap between the two vehicles like telepathic waves. Silas' right eye gleamed hotly, a burning star in the stone-like mask of his face, while his left eye—whatever remained of it anyway—was hidden beneath a black patch. He had to be in incredible pain. It had only been twenty-four hours since his eye had been shredded, but instead of recuperating in a hospital bed, Silas was out here hunting the one who had wounded him. Asher wondered how many narcotics he had jacked into his system in order to function.

Silas held the steering wheel in one hand, a Glock-17 in the other. The look on his face was one of grim finality and at that precise moment, Asher knew they had reached the end of the line. Something dark and cold seeped into his blood, a strange numbness that somehow hurt worse than any pain.

He punched the gas. Rubber screamed in protest as it peeled off the tires and pasted to the pavement in smoking stripes. Up ahead, the Tacoma did the same and the two trucks hurtled toward each other on a collision course. Rain whipped in through the shattered side windows and stabbed at Asher's eyes like icy needles. The two trucks closed the gap fast.

At the last possible second, Asher jerked the wheel to the right. The Tacoma flashed by, missing him by inches. Asher's pulse pounded but beneath it all was a sense of loss. One of them was going to die this morning and no matter who it was, neither of them would ever be the same again. Regardless of who turned out to be the last man standing in the end, the sins of the past had left their mark on them both.

Asher slammed the brakes and guided the Ford through a controlled skid so that it once again faced the Toyota, which had also swung around for another pass. He wiped the rain off his face, drew his HK45, and growled, "All right, Silas. Let's finish this."

As if on cue, the Tacoma surged forward.

Asher pinned the pedal to the floor.

The two vehicles devoured the road like a pair of buzz-saws, rapidly closing the gap between them. Asher steered with his right hand, his left gripping the HK, eyes slitted against the wind and rain razoring through the cab.

When the Tacoma was only thirty yards away, less than two seconds from impact, Asher leveled the .45 out the window and fired several rapid rounds at the Toyota's driver-side front tire. At least one of the bullets struck home and the tire exploded with a bang.

The Tacoma veered out of control, barely missing Asher's truck. Its rear end sloughed around, and Asher caught a glimpse of Silas fighting the wheel as the vehicle barreled toward the ditch. Rags of rubber shot everywhere, and sparks flew as the bare metal rim bit into the blacktop. Then the blacktop became the shoulder, and the shoulder became the ditch. The Tacoma nosed in at close to 40 mph. Metal crunched, dirt and debris geysered into the air, and the truck came to an abrupt, bone-shattering halt.

The same could not be said for Silas.

He obviously had not been wearing a seatbelt; when the Tacoma slammed head-on into the ditch, inertia flung him through the windshield in a spray of glass. He looked like a scarecrow pin-wheeling through the air, arms flailing against the rain and gravity.

Asher watched as the ground rushed up to meet Silas, sucking him down into a snarled hell-zone of half-rotted fence posts and badly rusted coils of barbed wire. He thrashed and twisted in midair like a cat hurled off a roof. But nothing could save him from landing in the tangled pile of wire.

Silas screamed in pain as the steel coils snapped around him. Barbs tattered his clothes and fish-hooked his flesh. The wire wrapped around his wrists like bracelets, chewing at the veins there. More strands whipped across his face, neck, legs, and chest. Silas struggled against the metallic cocoon, but the more he fought, the tighter the razored embrace became, hopelessly trapping him in a sharp steel web. Asher couldn't make out the exact nature of the wounds from here, but he could see a lot of blood. It was the kind of blood spillage that someone didn't walk away from. Silas finally lay still, apparently realizing that every movement just dug the rusty fangs in even deeper.

Asher parked the Ranger on the shoulder where Silas had run off the road. As he stepped out of the truck, he hunched his shoulders against the cold rain pelting down. The wipers continued to keep their metronomic beat as he scanned the long, flat stretch of road in both directions. There were no cars coming. He and Silas were alone.

Asher kept his gun ready as he approached, but it wasn't necessary—Silas wasn't going anywhere. Asher crossed the ditch in front of the wrecked Tacoma. Steam hissed out from under the accordioned hood. Cold rain sizzled on hot metal as he went and stood over Silas.

Silas stared up at him with his one good eye filled with pain. "Hey...Gabriel," he said, the words slow and thick from the blood on his lips.

"Don't talk," Asher said. The .45 hung loosely in his hand, down by his side. Stretched out under the gray skies like a crucified martyr, Silas had no shelter from the rain, which began to come down harder, diluting some of the blood from Silas' wounds. But not all of it. It would take a downpour to get rid of all the blood.

"Why...not? I'm gonna...die...anyway." A spasm racked Silas' body. He arched his back against the pain.

The movement caused the barbs to burrow further into his flesh.

Asher stood still and silent as a thousand memories flashed through his mind, all of them from better days. He saw the tiny trailer park in which he and Silas had grown up, the fields in which they had played, the schools they had attended, the cars they had driven, the girls they had loved, along with all the other sunny images of childhood that the mind never forgets, no matter what darkness comes after.

Shoulders hunched against the rain, Asher stared down at the man he had once called friend. Nameless emotions formed a cold, hard ball in the pit of his stomach.

Silas tried to smile and somehow, that was the most sickening thing yet. "Hey...Gabe," he said. "We...sure had some...good times...huh?"

Asher lifted his head and looked at the sky. Nothing but gray as far as the eye could see. The thick, swollen clouds hung motionless in the sky. He lowered his head and looked at Silas again. "Yeah," he said. "I guess we did."

"I really am...sorry...for what I did."

Asher told himself it was just rain on his face, but who was he kidding?

Silas started to say something else, but it turned into a groan. He clenched his teeth so hard that the muscles of his jaw stood out in stark relief. But as Asher lowered his eyes to Silas' most mortal injury, he couldn't blame him. The barbed wire had ripped open his belly and his insides bulged, wet and glistening, from the gaping gash.

Asher lifted his eyes back to Silas' face and saw the

utter hopelessness there. Silas knew he was a dead man, knew that his gut wound would kill him as surely as a bullet to the brain, but it would be a slow, agonizing death. In a world of bad ways to die, it was one of the worst. "Gabe," Silas gasped, "kill me...please...I'm begging you...I can't take...this pain...please."

Asher had expected the grim request. Not only because he would have asked for the same thing were the situation reversed, but because he knew Silas. Knew him the way you only know someone you have both cherished and hated.

Asher stood in the wind and rain and got soaked, but he felt nothing save the chaos in his soul. He tightened his grip on the .45, feeling the dark promise of its weight. Yesterday, killing Silas would have been about revenge and retribution. But what did it mean today?

Mercy?

No, Asher thought, *it means more than that*. Putting a bullet in Silas, granting his wish, would not just be about mercy—it would be about forgiveness. The bullet would absolve Silas of his betrayal, forgive him for what he had done. Asher searched his heart. Was he ready for that?

Without knowing the answer, he raised the .45 and pointed it at Silas. Rain streamed from the metal like bitter tears. Silas' one eye stared up at him with frightening force, silently pleading. Asher started to take up the trigger slack, but his finger trembled. He took several deep breaths and told himself to just get on with it and pull the trigger. But he didn't. He *couldn't*. He just stood there, unsure, and watched the blood spill from Silas' torn body.

Thunder boomed in the distance, its deep bass

rumble echoing off the mountains and rolling across the fields. It might have been an ominous portent, had Asher put faith in such things.

Silas flinched at the sound and the involuntary motion caused his exposed viscera to shift. Something long and wet unspooled to the ground. Silas screamed, shredding the air into aural splinters of agony, the single most wrenching scream Asher had ever heard.

Silas instinctively tried to press his hands over his ripped-open belly, forgetting that his wrists were held tight. He fought the barbed wire for a moment, flopping and thrashing desperately, but only managed to turn his wrists into even more of a mangled mess and make more of his internal organs become external ones.

He finally stopped, exhausted. "Gabriel...please...it hurts so bad...I'm begging you..."

Asher lowered the gun. "I can't," he said. "I just can't." The cold, hard knot in his guts had found its way into his throat.

Silas stared at him with eyes that were black pools of sorrow and pain. "Please, Gabe...it's just one more bullet."

Asher searched his soul for the rage and hatred that had sustained him for so long but found only an aching hollow. He gripped the .45 so tightly he thought he would crush it into scrap metal as he slowly raised the gun again.

He locked eyes with Silas one last time. "Rest in peace or rot in Hell. God's choice."

"Please...forgive me," Silas said.

Asher pulled the trigger, the sound of the shot lost in a sudden peal of thunder. As smoke bled from the barrel, Silas' pain ended, the forgiveness he had craved symbolized by the bullet hole in his heart. The blood looked black in the rain.

Asher walked slowly back to the truck. It was only when he was back behind the wheel that he allowed a single tear to scald his cheek.

CHAPTER 18

ASHER DROVE through the storm to Morningside Cemetery. Though only eight miles from where he and Silas had faced each other for the final time, it was raining a lot harder here, and the thunder rumbled with booming cracks that seemed like they would shatter the tombstones.

He left the truck at the gate and walked up the hill toward Karen's grave. Hard to believe he had been here only twelve hours ago. He touched the cut on his forehead, feeling the stitches to remind himself that this was all real, not just some nightmare conjured up by his psyche.

Yeah, this was real all right. Macklin was dead. Silas was dead. Larissa might or might not be dead. Death was all around. For a moment, Asher imagined he felt the Reaper's breath on the back of his neck. But no, that was just the wind.

The downpour prevented the leaves from crunching under his feet as he walked toward Karen's grave. Despite the early morning hour, the storm turned the world into twilight. Lightning slithered through the dark, bruised clouds and stabbed the earth with blue-white pitchforks. The rain hammered down fiercely, as if it had a grudge, the water droplets feeling more like stone pellets as he trudged through the maze of marble markers. Above him, the canopy of bare branches rattled together like ancient bones.

As he walked, the HK45 appeared in his hand. He didn't remember drawing it, but there it was, cold and heavy, as if placed there against his will by some unseen force. It brushed against the gravestones as he made his way among the dead.

When he reached Karen's grave, he knelt in front of the marker and brushed the raindrops from the inscription. The stone felt cool to the touch, but somehow comforting at the same time. Here, more than anywhere else, he felt close to his wife.

"God, Karen, I miss you so much." Emotion choked his throat, and tears christened the ground. But hope lay beyond his sorrow; he had come here to say goodbye, to free himself from the chains of the past and find a way to love again. For as he stood in that hospital room and watched Larissa cling to life, he had finally understood that life without love is not really life at all.

He looked at the .45. Once he had sought salvation in the gun, but now he knew it was nothing but a curse binding him to a destiny of lonely violence. When Karen died, he had amputated his emotions and replaced them with bullets and blood. He made death his life, his fate, his God, and allowed the scars to consume his soul. But he didn't want to live like that anymore.

Time to let go.

He ejected the HK's magazine and removed a single cartridge, holding it in his palm. He looked down at it as rain spackled the brass. Bullets were all he had known for a lot of years, but now it was time to say goodbye. He let the cartridge fall from his fingers.

The bullet landed on the muddy ground where it gleamed like the devil's eye. Asher imagined Karen in the grave below, reaching up with gentle fingers to take the bullet, to take away the past that the bullet represented, so that he would be free to start over again.

He slid the magazine back into the HK45. He considered leaving the gun here too, but he had too many enemies to walk around unarmed. The symbolism of the single bullet would have to suffice. He stood up and began walking back down the hill.

After a few steps, he turned back for one final look at Karen's grave, one last silent goodbye. At that moment, lightning scorched the sky, driving back the shadows from the tombstone, illuminating her name.

With a smile ghosting his lips, he turned and walked back to the truck with only the symphony of the storm to keep him company, knowing that every step was a journey toward salvation. For the first time in a long time, he actually believed that everything would be all right.

CHAPTER 19

ASHER DITCHED the Ford Ranger and stole another truck from the long-term lot of a train station. He did not return to the hospital right away. The place would be crawling with police and security personnel, a uniform at every entrance. Besides, it had only been two hours since he left; Larissa probably wasn't even out of surgery yet. Unless she was bagged and tagged on a slab in the morgue.

To keep those kinds of thoughts at bay, he drove aimlessly, passing time, making random turns over roads he had known since childhood. He passed farms that had been built before he was born and would probably still be standing after he died. He passed rolling pastures dotted with wet cows huddled together against the rain and cornfields bent nearly flat by the wind. He passed the old red and white trailer that had been home to the first girl he ever kissed. Everywhere he went, he passed another landmark, another memory around every bend. He hadn't lived around here for over twenty years, but somehow it still felt like home.

Around noon, he pulled into the tiny hamlet of Adamsville, one of those blink-and-you'll-miss-it spots on the map and stopped at a little country store. The wind had eased up, but the rain continued to come down in buckets and he got soaked to the bone as he ran inside to grab some food and water. He then parked near a pair of gas pumps that looked like they had been modern when horse-and-buggies were still in vogue and took his time eating.

When he was done, he dug out his cell phone. As rain drummed loudly on the roof, he looked up a number and dialed. A cheerful female voice answered, "Thank you for calling Glens Falls Hospital. How may I help you?"

"I need to speak to Dr. Morrow."

"One moment."

Asher stared out the window while Muzak polluted his ear. Off in the distance, over toward the mountains, it looked like the storm was finally breaking up, the sky lightening. After what seemed like a long time but was probably less than a minute, he heard a click, followed by, "Dr. Morrow speaking."

And just like that, the moment arrived. He was about to find out if Larissa was alive or dead. He steeled himself, not sure what he would do if Morrow told him Larissa had not pulled through. Taking a deep breath, he plunged ahead. "Dr. Morrow, you don't know who I am, but I brought a woman in this morning with a gunshot wound to her temple and I'm trying to find out—"

"Is this Mr. Asher?"

Asher gripped the phone a little tighter. "How do you know my name?"

"You're pretty much all Larissa has talked about."

"She's alive?" Asher could hear the relief in his own voice.

"Alive and doing very well. Especially for someone who took a bullet to the head."

Asher clutched the phone, unable to speak.

"I'll spare you the technical jargon and medical mumbo jumbo," Morrow continued. "Let's just say that the bullet ricocheted off her skull. Tore a nasty gash in her scalp and chipped some bone, but all things considered, she is a very lucky young lady. Taking a bullet to the head, *twice*, and surviving...well, that the closest thing to a miracle I've ever witnessed."

Thinking over everything that had happened the last few days, Asher said, "Sometimes fate just has other plans."

"Guess so," Morrow replied. "But I still wouldn't advise her to a try it a third time. By the way, she keeps asking for you."

"Tell her I'll be there as soon as I can."

Asher hung up and stared out the window as he processed the information. Larissa was alive. Maybe fate was finally done being a cruel, vicious bitch.

He fired up the truck and headed toward the hospital. He pictured Larissa lying under cool, clean sheets, waiting for him.

Every mile seemed like an eternity, an eternity filled with sheets of rain and slick roads. When he hit the Flats, he saw pulsing police lights up ahead about a half-mile. They had found Silas' body. Asher imagined him lying there, stretched out on the barbed wire like a crucified scarecrow as cops, coroners, and crime scene technicians scurried about.

Asher reached for his .45, hand closing around the handle of the HK. It was an instinctive action, one that might never fully go away, no matter how hard he tried to put a life of blood and bullets behind him. It suddenly seemed like there were police cars everywhere, swarms of them, all waiting to surround him, drag him from the truck, slap on the cuffs, and haul him away to some dark, dingy prison cell.

Asher took his foot off the gas. Indecision wrenched at him. Every fiber of his being screamed at him to turn around. To just run away and accept the bleakness of his past rather than risk the uncertain hope of the future.

But no. There was no turning back. He didn't know what lay ahead, but he knew he didn't want to live without Larissa. Turning back now would be like turning his back on her and that was something he vowed never to do again.

So he put his foot back on the gas and continued down the road. A young cop, soaked right down to the socks and looking pissed to be out in this miserable weather, motioned him around all the emergency vehicles and moments later the police—and his indecision—were behind him.

Twenty minutes later, he pulled into the hospital's short-term parking lot. He found a spot near the back and turned off the engine but remained in the truck. The rain had slackened but was still coming down, though not enough to ruin visibility. Asher settled back in his seat and surveyed the hospital entrance for several minutes, studying the human traffic, alert for anyone that looked like a badge. Seeing no threat, he began to relax.

He leaned forward and looked up at the rows of windows that made up the face of the hospital, wondering which one was Larissa's room. Hard to believe she still loved him after all these years, all the things he had done, all the blood he had spilled. None of that mattered to her. She had forgiven him for sins he wasn't sure he would ever fully forgive himself.

He looked up at the gray sky. The clouds showed signs of breaking up, but the light rain continued to drizzle. He scanned the area one more time but saw nothing that raised his hackles, so he exited the truck, his boots splashing down in about an inch of water. He hunched his shoulders to keep the rain from slipping under his collar, and then stepped out from between the row of parked vehicles.

He saw the gunmen a half-second too late. One moment, nothing; the next, a shadowy blur of movement between two cars. Asher barely registered the threat before the bullet took him in the left shoulder, drilling clean through. The world spun crazily as the sudden impact whipped him around and draped him over the hood of a white sedan. As he slowly pushed himself back up, the pain smacked his system, sharp and hot and throbbing. He could see his blood spattered across the car.

Grimacing, he turned to see two gunmen aiming Heckler & Koch MP5 submachine guns at him. Sound suppressors and laser sighting systems adorned the weapons. Asher glanced down and saw two small red dots glowing on the center of his chest. He looked back up, gaze flicking back and forth between the gunners. The hole in his shoulder felt like somebody had run him through with a red-hot poker. "Who are you?" he asked.

The men held the MP5s with the confident ease of hunters who know they have their target dead to rights. "It'll all be explained in a minute," the one on the left said. "First, get rid of your gun. Take it out, two fingers only, nice and slow."

Asher complied. Wasn't like he had any other options. Wounded and pinned down like this, any offensive or defensive action would be a suicide play. The full auto guns would cut him down in a heartbeat. All he could do was see how things played out. He tossed the HK45 onto the hood of the white sedan.

"Good boy," the gunner said. "Now just stand there and bleed."

Asher felt blood running down his body from the entry and exit holes in his shoulder, streams of heat in sharp contrast to the cold rain.

A black SUV, all sleek surfaces, polished gleam, and darkened windows, rounded the corner like a living thing, tires parting the puddles. Asher watched it glide forward like a shark until it came to a stop close enough for him to see his reflection in the tinted glass. The gunners across the way edged to his right, keeping the red dots firmly painted on his sternum.

Asher ignored them. Right now, for some reason, the SUV seemed more menacing than the gunmen. A chill that had nothing to do with the rain crept through him. Tension punched his guts with a cold, bony fist.

The front doors of the vehicle swung open with a slow deliberateness. Two more gunners—one the driver, one riding shotgun—emerged, both sporting chiseled features and sound-suppressed, laser-equipped MP5 submachine guns. The driver painted another red dot on Asher's chest, promising death and destruction if he so much as twitched. The other gunman circled around and opened the driver's side passenger door, backed away a yard or so, and leveled his weapon as well. Asher didn't need to look down to know that a fourth red dot had joined the others on his center mass.

A moment later, Rene Perelli stepped out of the SUV.

She was a few inches taller than Asher remembered. But that probably had something to do with the stiletto heels she wore. They made a sharp clicking sound when they hit the pavement. But her height was not the only thing different about her, Asher noted. When he had seen her earlier this week, right before putting a bullet into Peter Perelli, she had been a sobbing, pleading, weeping wreck. But now, only days after burying her husband, Rene Perelli practically oozed confidence. It oozed from the striking white dress and matching wide-brimmed hat she wore. It oozed from the demeanor of her stance, a queen surveying her subjects. But more than anything else, confidence oozed from her eyes.

Eyes that stared at Asher with unbridled hatred.

Rain ran off the brim of her hat like a veil. Asher felt her hate, a black, palpable presence bridging the gap between them, driving the coldness even deeper into his bones. He tried not to think about Larissa. With one bullet hole in him already and four guns pointed at his chest, he had to face the fact that he might not walk away from this one, might not get a chance to see her again. The thought was almost more than he could stand.

Rene Perelli's smile looked like the curved edge of a

scimitar. "Hello, Asher. I've been looking forward to meeting you again."

Her beauty still had the power to stun, but with a more primal edge. Before, her beauty had been that of a frail, vulnerable dove; now she possessed the beauty of a hunting wolf—relentless and unforgiving. Asher's hopes for survival plummeted.

"What's wrong, Asher? Nothing to say?" Rene's voice sounded light and amused, a tigress toying with her prey.

"I'll say anything you want if you tell your boys to point those guns somewhere else."

Rene laughed, but like everything else about her, the laugh had a dark edge. "Sorry, but I'm afraid I can't do that."

"Never hurts to ask." Asher gauged the distance between himself and Rene. If he could grab the mob queen before her goons opened fire, this would be a whole new ballgame. But no, it was too far. He'd be riddled by a dozen slugs before he even got close. Desperation began to prowl the edges of his mind. "So, what's this about?"

Rene's eyes flashed dangerously. "Don't be coy, Asher. You know full well what this is about." She reached into the left-hand pocket of her dress and pulled out a white rose with blood-stained petals. "Recognize it? You should. It's the rose you dropped on my husband's body after you killed him." Her tone was icy-hot. "After you left, I crawled across the floor to Peter, picked up this rose, and swore I would lay it on your dead body."

Asher stared at the black, crusted blood on the rose's once-pure petals and felt regret knife through

him. He thought of a thousand things to say to the grieving, vengeful widow in front of him, but the words
would just be wasted breath. So in the end, all he said
was, "If I could take it all back, I would, but I can't."

Tears glistened in Rene Perelli's eyes. "No, you
can't," she said softly. "I loved my husband, and you
took him from me. My little girl loved her daddy, and
you took him away from her. There is nothing on the
face of this earth that you can do to atone for that day. I
want you dead, Asher. I want you dead so bad I can
taste it." She paused for a moment, as if savoring the
thought of him rotting six feet under, and then said,
"But instead, I'm going to give you a choice, a choice
you didn't give me."

"What kind of choice?" Asher asked.

"The impossible kind." Still holding the rose in her
left hand, Rene reached into her coat pocket with the
right hand and pulled out her cell phone. "I have a text
typed out that says 'Kill her'. All I have to do is press
'Send' and the man I have waiting in the lobby will
receive that text and immediately proceed to the fourth
floor, room number four-oh-six, where he will execute
your beloved Larissa."

Asher forgot all about his pain as horror locked a
choking grip around his throat. He pictured Larissa
lying in her hospital bed as a man pressed a silenced
pistol to her temple and pulled the trigger. At point-
blank range, the caliber wouldn't matter; any bullet
would be enough to kill her. Asher imagined the fear
and terror she would feel right before she died.

He locked eyes with Rene and said, "You heartless
bitch."

"I called you a heartless bastard the night you

executed my husband," Rene reminded him. "It didn't stop you from blowing his brains out, so do you really think calling me a heartless bitch is going to save your girlfriend?"

"Then tell me how," Asher said. "Tell me how to save her."

Dried blood flaked off the rose petals and stained Rene's fingers. "One of you lives, one of you dies," she said. "But I leave the choice up to you. I send the text and my man puts a bullet in her brain. You'll get to live, but it will be without her."

"What's the second option?"

Rene gestured at the four gunmen pinning him with their lasers. "They pump you full of bullets and Larissa gets to live, but she'll have to do it without *you*. Any way you look at it, the story of Asher and Larissa will not have a happy ending."

Asher didn't even have to think about it. There was no choice at all. He would gladly trade his life for hers. "You know what my choice is," he said to Rene. "Do what you want to me but give me your word that she lives."

Rene gazed at him for several moments and then nodded. She slipped the cell phone back into her pocket. "You have my word, but on one condition." She stepped forward and held the rose out to him. "I want you to hold that while you die."

Realizing the tactical error, the gunman closest to Rene called out, "Ma'am, don't—"

Too late.

Gritting his teeth against the burning pain in his wounded shoulder, Asher snaked out his left hand, bypassing the rose to grab Rene's wrist. He yanked her forward, causing her to stumble in her stiletto heels, putting her body between him and the gunners. No way in hell would they risk taking a shot that might strike their master.

At the same time, he raised his right leg and used his free hand to pluck the Gerber Guardian Back Up dagger from its hidden boot sheath. He spun Rene around so that she faced her men and laid the razored edge of the blade against the artery pulsing just beneath the fragile skin of her throat. Just a few more ounces of pressure would send a scarlet fountain spurting into the rain.

"Don't make me kill you," he growled into her ear. "Tell your boys to drop their weapons."

"Never!" she hissed; her defiance undiminished.

"Do you want to die?"

"You cut my throat, they'll gun you down two seconds later."

Asher knew she spoke the truth. As if to prove her point, two of the gunmen edged to the side, one going left, one going right, clearly thinking about a flanking maneuver. If they managed to circle to his peripheral, he would be exposed. Bullets would rip into his ribcage and he would be down for the count, checkmate, game over. He didn't have much time.

"Think of your daughter," he said to Rene. "Do you want her to grow up without a father *or* mother? Tell those assholes to drop their guns."

"Go to hell," she snarled. "Don't act like you give a shit about my daughter." She raised her voice to her bodyguards. "Somebody kill this son of a bitch! Shoot through me if that's what it takes."

The two in-motion gunners continued sidestepping

toward his flanks, but no one fired. Nobody had a clear shot yet. Despite her orders, they refused to shoot through their boss to take out the target. But Asher knew the numbers were fast running down to zero.

"Last chance." He rasped the words through pain-clenched teeth. "Don't make me cut your throat."

"Go ahead," Rene said. "You already cut out my heart."

Without warning, Asher shoved her toward the flanking gunner on his right, blocking the man's line of fire. At the same time, he dove to the left, landing on the hood of the white sedan, snatching up the HK45 as he slid across the rain- and blood-slicked metal. As momentum carried him over the other side, he managed to snap off two quick shots at the other flanking gunner. The first bullet flew wide but the second one drilled into the man's right eye and cored open his brain.

Asher landed on the pavement in a painful, grace-less heap as the remaining three gunmen opened up on full auto. The 9mm fusillades shredded the sedan, tattooing the metalwork, popping the tires, and punching the glass into shattered cubes. Asher kept the car's engine block between him and the salvos, knowing it would take something heavier than a 9mm round to pierce the thick steel.

Professional operators would have reacted more swiftly to his evasive action and probably cut him down before he finished skidding across the hood of the sedan. But despite the tactical weapons and top-tier laser sights, these guys were still just your basic, run-of-the-mill mob goons. Asher had banked on that, had rolled the life-and-death dice that their reaction time would be slow enough to give him an opening, and it had paid off.

Now he just had to kill them all.

One down, three to go.

The instant there was a lull in the enemy's fire, he popped up from behind the bullet-riddled car like a pistol-packing jack-in-the-box. He smoked the nearest gunman with a double tap to the chest, the suppressed .45 slugs kicking the guy right off his feet. He immediately dropped back down behind the sedan. One of the two surviving bodyguards blasted off a short burst, the slugs thudding into the car with a staccato, metallic *thwack-thwack-thwack* sound.

Asher cursed every passing second. By now, Rene Perelli had most likely sent the text ordering Larissa executed. Which meant that every moment he spent pinned down here, shooting it out with these mob hitters, carved away at Larissa's chances of survival. If he wanted to have any chance in hell of saving her, he needed to end this fast.

He leaned out around the car's fender just in time to see one of the two remaining gunmen pulling Rene Perelli to her feet. She must have fallen to the ground when Asher threw her. The other bodyguard circled behind the SUV, using it for concealment. He borrowed a page from Asher's defensive playbook, sheltering behind the engine block.

Too bad for him he left the lower part of his left leg exposed.

Asher prostrated himself on the pavement and got his sights on the target. He hit the HK's trigger and sent a single bullet sizzling beneath the SUV and into the man's ankle. Hot lead smashed into hard bone and blew everything apart.

With a howled curse of pain, the gunner fell onto his side, clutching at the agonizing wound. Asher ended his suffering with a quick shot to the head that sprayed chunks of his skull across the rain-drenched asphalt.

Gritting his teeth and powering through the pain in his shoulder, Asher surged to his feet and swung his HK over the roof of the sedan toward the last of Rene Perelli's security detail. The bodyguard had Rene's head pushed down as he hustled her toward the SUV, keeping his body between her and the threat at their back.

The gunner wielded the MP5 one-handed, triggering a blind burst back over his shoulder without even looking. He wasn't really trying to hit anything; just wanted to keep Asher at bay long enough to secure his master—followed by himself—in the armored, bullet-resistant vehicle.

Asher had no intention of letting that happen.

The .45 bucked in his hand.

The bullet struck the bodyguard in the back of his neck. Hunched over like she was, Rene just missed getting clipped by the exiting slug as it exploded out the man's throat in a spray of blood and ruptured vertebrae.

Killed on his feet, the man's dead weight lurched forward and drove Rene's head into the side of the SUV. She bounced off the dented metal and sprawled on the wet pavement, dazed but conscious. Her lifeless bodyguard hit the ground and slid under the vehicle, asphalt grinding his unfeeling face to mangled hash.

Asher emerged from behind the sedan and swiftly closed in on Rene as she pulled herself up into a sitting position against the SUV's rear tire, shaking her head to clear the fog. The blood-crusted rose lay where she had dropped it and Asher crushed it under his boot as he moved in.

He dropped to one knee next to her and pressed the tip of the HK45's suppressor against her breastbone. He looked into her eyes and she looked back, unflinching, unwavering, asking no quarter. One more pull of the trigger and it would be over.

But he stayed his hand.

He wanted a fresh start at life, not another kill on his conscience.

"What are you waiting for?" Rene hissed. "Just do it and get it over with."

"I don't want to kill you." To prove it, Asher removed the gun from her chest. "I took your husband's life and for that I'm sorry. But now I'm letting you have your life. Let this war end right here, right now." A fresh bolt of pain seared through his shoulder.

She searched his eyes, seeking the truth, and found it.

She nodded. "Deal." Then she took her hand out of her pocket and held up her cell phone, showing him the screen. "But your woman still dies."

The text—the execution order—had been sent and read.

Teeth clenched, Asher thudded the .45 back against her sternum with enough force to bruise the bone. Something inside his scarred-up soul let out a bestial roar, begging him to slam a slug through her heart and be done with it. But the other part, the part awakened by Larissa, warned him that the path to redemption could not be paved with bullets and blood.

His finger trembled on the trigger for a few flickering heartbeats, but then he pulled the gun away again.

"Go home," he rasped. "Take care of your daughter. But if I ever see you again, if you ever come after me or anyone I love, I will not hesitate, I will not be merciful. I'll kill you dead in your tracks. Let there be no doubt about that."

He didn't wait for a response. Just stood up and ran through the storm toward the hospital without a backward glance. Rene Perelli represented the sins of his past. Larissa represented the hope for a better future.

If it wasn't already too late.

He rushed through the hospital's main entrance with the desperation of the damned, rain streaming off him as he charged toward the stairway. Rene Perelli's henchman had the advantage of a head-start, but he had most likely taken the elevator. With luck, the car would have to stop at multiple floors. By taking the stairs, Asher might be able to gain some ground.

He barreled through the door that led to the stairway and took the steps three at a time. Fourth floor, room 406, Perelli had said. His shoulder screamed in pain, but he ignored it.

He reached the fourth floor and exited the stairway to find himself at the end of a long hallway of hospital rooms. Assorted medical equipment formed an obstacle course in the corridor and the air smelled like antiseptic.

Asher glanced at the nearest room. The sign above the door read 410.

His eyes scanned ahead and glimpsed a large, hulking man in a long trench-coat turn into room 406.

The man's right hand delved inside his coat as he walked in, as if reaching for a shoulder-holstered pistol.

Asher powered forward, fueled by desperate, adrenalized fury. He sprinted down the hall, leaving droplets of blood behind him, drawing the HK45 on the run. A nurse screamed and dropped an IV bag as he raced by. Somewhere a patient cried out in terror.

This sanctuary of healing was about to become a kill-zone.

Asher turned the corner into room 406 with the HK raised, leveled, and looking for the threat.

The trench-coated killer was a goliath, at least six-foot-six, with linebacker shoulders that looked wide as an oak tree. He towered over Larissa as he brought a suppressed SIG Sauer P226 pistol to bear on her left temple as she lay on the hospital bed, her head swaddled in a gauze bandage.

"Who's there?" Asher heard her ask, fear causing her voice to tremble.

The .45 bucked in Asher's fist, twice in rapid succession, both shots fired into the man's back without shame. To hell with honor. This was about survival.

The brutal, short-range impacts punched the man forward. His knees caught the edge of the bed and he toppled across Larissa's legs, then tumbled over the other side. Larissa let out a cry. Asher heard the guy grunt when he hit the floor. His blood spackled the clean, white sheets.

Asher moved forward, but before he reached Larissa, the henchman powered upright with a bellowed roar of rage and pain. He still had the gun in his hand.

No fucking way! Asher couldn't believe it. Blood

poured from a pair of exit wounds in the killer's chest. The bastard had no right to be alive, let alone on his feet.

The henchman started to swing his pistol back into play. Not aiming for Larissa this time, but going for Asher...

...who double-tapped two more slugs into his chest.

The rounds punched all the way through the killer's body and drilled into the window behind him. Hot blood and flecks of lung tissue spattered the weakened glass as cracks radiated out from the bullet holes in a jagged spider-web pattern.

The man staggered backward, but still refused to go down. He stared at Asher, lips peeled back in an animalistic snarl, baring blood-stained teeth. More blood from his punctured lungs seeped from the corners of his mouth and dripped off his jowls. Despite being damn near dead on his feet, he still tried to raise the SIG, like some kind of cyborg that would not give up until he completed his termination mission.

"Will you just fucking die?" Asher rasped, hitting the trigger one more time.

The .45 slug hammered the henchman square in the face. His head whiplashed back with so much force that his neck snapped. The high-powered impact punched him right out the cracked window in a spray of glass shards that glittered like razored diamonds in the drizzling rain. Turned from killer to corpse in a single heartbeat, the man made no sound as he vanished into the darkness. Asher didn't actually hear the *splat-crunch* of the body crash-landing on the concrete four stories below, but it wasn't hard to imagine.

He rushed to Larissa's side and carefully gathered

her into his arms, careful not to jostle her bandaged head. His bullet-pierced shoulder throbbed with protesting pain, but he ignored it. His wounds didn't matter, not right now, not when he had come so close to losing her. If he had shown up just a second or two later, the hitter would have put that final bullet into her head. The grim thought was almost more than he could stand.

Larissa clutched at him, tears on her face. "Gabriel? Is that you? What's happening?"

There wasn't enough time to tell her everything he wanted to say. To tell her that she had saved him from his own personal hell. To tell her that he no longer wanted to live without her, imprisoned in a world where the guns forever thundered, and the bullets forever flew.

He would tell her all that at another time. Right now, he just wanted—*needed*—her to hear four words.

"I love you, Larissa."

He kissed her and for a moment, time stopped.

But the moment couldn't last forever.

"I have to go," he said. "But I promise you I'll be back."

Larissa held him tighter. "No. Please, Gabriel, don't leave me. Not now."

"I have to," he said. "If I stay here, they'll put me in a cage."

"I don't want to lose you." A sob caught in Larissa's throat. "Not again, not after all this."

"You're not going to lose me," Asher said. "I'll find you; I promise."

He meant every word. Not just a simple promise, but a sacred vow. Not even the fires of hell would keep him from finding his way back to her. If he had learned anything these last few days, it was that destiny would not be denied.

The sound of sirens floated through the shattered window as he turned and quickly left the room. He didn't dare risk a backward glance, knowing that if he turned around, he might never be able to leave. The sound of Larissa weeping as he walked away tore at his heart.

Outside, he scanned the parking lot. Rene Perelli and the black SUV were nowhere in sight. Her bodyguards lay where they had fallen. He prayed, for both their sakes, that she heeded his warning and never crossed his path again.

He skirted the edge of the crowd of gawkers gathered around the broken body of the man who had nearly murdered Larissa. The corpse was a bloody mess, haloed in a crimson pool. The gore-ghouls had their phones out, snapping pictures.

Nobody paid Asher any attention as he kept to the shadows, moving away from the hospital. Head down, collar up, he was nothing but a featureless ghost shuffling down the sidewalk by the time the police cars rolled into the parking lot, lights strobing the rain-soaked night with blurred pulses of color.

His breath plumed in the cold like dragon-smoke. The bullet wound in his shoulder hurt like hell, but it paled in comparison to the ache he felt at having to leave Larissa behind. He prayed to whatever angels might be listening to keep her safe until he found his way back to her side.

CHAPTER 20

SIX WEEKS LATER...

LARISSA WAS JUST GETTING ready to eat the brownie from her microwave dinner when she heard the sound of a vehicle rolling up the driveway, snow-covered gravel crunching under the tires. The sound easily carried on the crisp air of the night. Though she couldn't see them, she imagined headlights flashing across the windows of the trailer, illuminating the panes of glass beyond the drawn curtains.

She quickly moved the TV tray aside, then reached down on the couch beside her and picked up the pump-action shotgun. Her thumb found the safety and flicked it off. No need to rack the slide—there was already a shell riding in the chamber. She suspected, given the tragic turns her life had taken, that there would *always* be one in the chamber.

She had found the shotgun in the bedroom closet of the ramshackle trailer she had rented just outside the tiny hamlet of Vesper Falls, way up in the northern

Adirondack Mountains, just a short hop from the Canadian border. It had been advertised as a hunting lodge, so no lease or background checks or any of the nonsense that might help someone track down her whereabouts. In reality, it was just a '70's-era singlewide perched on cement blocks. But it was set well back from the road on 15 acres of rough terrain, with a widespread swamp forming a natural barrier to the north and east while thick woods bracketed her western perimeter. Her nearest neighbor lived over a mile up the road, granting her all the privacy she could afford on her limited funds.

Despite Dr. Morrow's protests, the police had grilled her for several days while she recuperated in the hospital bed. The events that made Asher look heroic, she told them; the ones that made him seem like a rogue, trigger-happy assassin, she left out or glossed over. None of it mattered. By the time the local detectives were replaced by federal agents in black suits and stern expressions, it was blatantly clear the authorities wanted nothing more than to throw Asher in a cage—or more likely, an unmarked grave. He had been right to run, even though it had broken her heart.

But eventually all the badges went away, and she checked herself out of the hospital, despite Dr. Morrow protesting he wanted to keep her under observation for another few days. She took a taxi to the bus station and booked a ticket north, disembarking in the mountain town of Saranac Lake. She suspected the Company had slapped a tail on her in case Asher showed up, but her blindness made it impossible to be sure, so she didn't fret about it much. She trusted that Asher would come back for her and when he did, he would deal with any trackers in his own way.

The local librarian had been happy to help out a handicapped woman and put her in touch with a man named Ernie Foxx who rented hunting cabins—or in her case, hunting trailer—and had graciously driven her out here, even stopping along the way so she could pick up some groceries.

But unless she was very much mistaken, it wasn't Ernie rolling up the driveway. She was all paid up for the next two months and had made it very clear that she wanted to be left alone.

She heard a vehicle door slam shut—whoever the visitor was, they weren't being stealthy about their arrival—followed by the telltale sound of footsteps crunching in the snow outside. Winter came early up here in God's country.

She touched the shotgun's muzzle to the trailer's main door, about waist high. Given all she had been through, she wouldn't need much reason to pull the trigger and blast whoever was on the other side of the door clean in half with a buckshot bisection.

But not yet. First, she had to make sure it wasn't just some persistent Jehovah's Witness or vacuum cleaner salesman.

She heard footsteps coming up the creaky metal stairs to the small porch outside the door. They were heavy steps, almost stomping, as if whoever owned the feet doing the stepping wanted to make damn sure she could hear them coming. Not exactly the ninja-like stealth of an assassin.

Still, she refused to let down her guard. She almost racked the slide for emphasis but decided against it. She might need every shell the gun could hold. She curled her finger against the trigger and called out in a challenging voice, "Who are you?"

A bemused chuckle came from the other side of the thin, metal door. "I'm guessing you've got a blaster pointed at my guts right now."

"Damn right I do," Larissa replied. "And if you don't tell me who you are in about two seconds, I'm putting some buckshot in your belly."

Another chuckle. "Asher warned me you might be feeling feisty. Don't shoot, lady. I'm a friendly."

At the mention of his name, Larissa felt the breath catch in her throat. But she kept her voice low and hard as she snapped, "I still haven't heard your name."

"My name is Malakai. Asher sent me. I'm here to take you to him."

Malakai. Gabriel's old partner.

"How do I know I can trust you?"

"If I wanted you dead..."

Larissa smiled knowingly and lowered the shotgun. "Yeah...I'd be dead already."

"Exactly."

She opened the door. A risk, sure, but to be with Asher, it was a risk worth taking. Cold air drifted in and raised gooseflesh on her arms.

She stepped back. "Maybe you should come on in and tell me what the plan is."

Malakai closed the door behind him, shutting out the cold night. "Thanks for not filling me full of holes," he said. "Much appreciated."

"Don't mention it. How long have you been in the area?"

"Since yesterday."

"Notice anyone keeping tabs on me?"

"Couple of Company boys."

"You deal with them?"

"They've been neutralized. That gives us a window to get the hell out of here without anyone following us. I've got new papers for you, a new passport, the whole nine yards. Your old life is over. Time to start a new one."

"With Gabriel."

"Yeah."

"Where are we going?"

"Someplace a lot warmer than here."

"As long as it's not Hell."

"No." She could hear sympathy in Malakai's voice. "You and Asher have already been there."

———

Barra de Potosi, Guerrero, Mexico

Asher watched the sun as it began its descent below the horizon, the bottom edge of the orange ball of fire just starting to kiss the ocean where it blended with the blue-shadowed sky. A breathtaking sight, one that never got old.

Further up the beach, concealed by the curve of the land, the local townsfolk would be visiting the open-air, thatch-roofed *enramadas* that lined the lagoon for fresh fish and seafood. But even in a remote fishing village populated by less than 1,000 inhabitants, Asher had sought even greater seclusion. Thankfully, in this place, isolation was just a short walk away.

He had no plans to stay here forever—Australia or Switzerland seemed like better long-term options—but

Barra de Potosi seemed like a good spot to lay low while any heat from the Company or the Perelli organization subsided.

And while he waited for Malakai to track down Larissa and smuggle her across the border.

A soft, salt-tanged breeze cooled his skin as he stared off into the distance, watching the setting sun christen the waters with rays of red and gold. The sand beneath his feet felt warm and soothing. Out here, on what felt like the edge of the world, it was hard to imagine he would ever need the .45 tucked into the small of his back, hidden beneath a thin, long-tailed cotton shirt.

This was not a village that asked many questions, but one of the old men in town had spotted the gun once and asked, "Why do you feel the need for a *pistola* here, amigo?"

"Even paradise has its snakes," Asher had replied.

The old man had nodded, then said, "Only the ones you bring with you."

"I won't be here long."

The old man nodded again. "Just make sure when you leave, you take your *serpientes* with you."

Asher smiled at the memory. The village had accepted his presence these last six weeks, but it had been a distant, arm's-length acceptance, void of any sense of welcome. They were a people of peace and he was clearly a man of war. They would not be sorry to see him leave and take his troubles with him.

Not much longer now.

The sun was half-gone below the horizon when he heard two sets of footsteps approaching in the sand behind him. His smile broadened when he turned to see Larissa holding onto Malakai's arm as he guided her down the beach. His heart warmed at the sight of her.

He waited until she was just a few steps away before he breathed her name. "Larissa..."

"Gabriel?" With a sob of relief and joy, she threw herself into his arms.

Time ceased to exist as they held each other. The kiss that followed was the sweetest he had ever known. A kiss for the wounded, a kiss of redemption, a kiss of destiny.

By the time the moment finally ended, Malakai had retreated far down the beach. He looked back and raised a hand in farewell. Asher did the same. He owed the man more than he could ever repay and it went unspoken between them that Malakai could call on his friend at any time and Asher would be there for him.

Larissa leaned into him, the ocean breeze caressing her hair, the glow of the dying sun soft on her face. "Promise me," she said, "that no matter what happens, we'll always be together."

Asher held her close and said, "I promise."

Hand in hand, as the shadows lengthened and the night birds started to sing, they walked down the lonely stretch of sand. Asher knew they would forever be hunted, forever live with crosshairs on their back. There would always be someone out there carrying bullets with their names on them. He had walked away from his old life, but only a fool would think it was that easy. But whatever tribulations they still had to face, whatever hells were still to come, at least they had each other.

For them, it was enough.

A LOOK AT BOOK TWO: THE ASSASSIN'S BETRAYAL

BY MARK ALLEN

HARD-HITTING PULP ACTION – AS THE BULLETS BLAZE IN A SCORCHED EARTH SHOWDOWN THEY'LL DISCOVER WHAT TRULY MATTERS MOST.

In the cold, lonely world of hired guns, Malakai is a legendary trigger-puller. The victim of a twisted, abusive childhood that left him both physically and emotionally scarred, blood and bullets have become his religion. Once partnered with Gabriel Asher before he walked away, Malakai stayed with the Company, honing his lethal skills to become the quintessential lone wolf assassin.

When he is contracted to stop the Syndicate—a powerful Japanese crime organization—from blackmailing the chairperson of the Senate Intelligence Committee, Malakai discovers someone is playing Judas and he needs to flush them out before he gets burned.

As the chaos and carnage escalate, his life gets complicated by the arrival of a mysterious woman who may have even more scars on her soul than he does. But is she really who she says she is? With betrayal all around him, Malakai knows one wrong move could cost him his life.

When the Syndicate hires a ruthless assassin named Jesus to hunt him down, Malakai knows the only way to survive is to fight fire with hellfire.

AVAILABLE JULY 2025

ABOUT THE AUTHOR

Mark Allen was raised by an ancient clan of ruthless ninjas and now that he has revealed this dark secret, he will most likely be dead by tomorrow for breaking the sacred oath of silence. The ninjas take this stuff very seriously.

He started writing "guns 'n' guts" (his term for the action genre) at the not-so-tender age of 16 and soon won his first regional short story contest. His debut action novel, The Assassin's Prayer, was optioned by Showtime for a direct-to-cable movie. When that didn't pan out, he published the book on Amazon to great success, moving over 10,000 copies in its first year.

Mark currently resides in the Adirondack Mountains of upstate New York with a wife who doubts his ninja skills because he's always slicing his fingers while chopping veggies, two daughters who refuse to take tae kwon do, let alone ninjitsu, and enough firepower to ensure that he is never bothered by door-to-door salesmen.